A Princess Rescue

Holly & Kelly Willoughby

Orion
Children's Books

First published in Great Britain in 2016
by Hodder and Stoughton

1 3 5 7 9 10 8 6 4 2

Text copyright © Holly and Kelly Willoughby 2016
The moral rights of the authors have been asserted.

A CIP catalogue record for this book is available from the British Library.

ISBN 978 1 4440 1459 4

Printed and bound in Great Britain by Clays Ltd, St Ives plc.

The paper and board used in this book are from well-managed forests
and other responsible sources.

Orion Children's Books
An imprint of Hachette Children's Group
Part of Hodder and Stoughton
Carmelite House
50 Victoria Embankment
London EC4Y 0DZ
An Hachette UK Company

www.hachette.co.uk

www.hachettechildrens.co.uk

Have you ever had a dream, Story-seeker?
A dream you think can't possibly come true?
Don't give up! If you can dream, you can achieve.
Anything is possible – no matter who you are, or
what you think is against you. Reach for the stars!

Contents

Welcome back, Story-seeker, to another glorious term at L'Etoile, School for Stars. The sun is shining and our girls are back together for the last term of the school year, in search of some serious fun!

Excitement explodes before they've even had a chance to unpack their bags, with the arrival of a mystery VIP. Who is she? A pop star? An actress? Royalty? Our L'Etoilettes soon realise that someone's out to get this new student and it's up to them to deliver her from disaster! If anyone can do it, our girls can, Story-seeker, so jump in and join the rescue team!

Love
Holly and Kelly Willoughby x

1

A Good Old Catch Up

'Twinkle!' Molly exclaimed as she opened the car door before it had even stopped outside L'Etoile.

'It's as if she's been waiting for us all!' Maria said, running round to join the cuddled-up pile of black fur and blonde ringlets on the front steps.

'Hi, girls!' Mr Hart said, walking across the drive in his gardening boots. 'How were your hols? I think Twinkle missed you more than ever this time!'

'Hi, Mr Hart!' Maria said. 'Great, thanks, but we've missed Twinkle-toes no end. We'll have to borrow her for the whole holidays one of these days – but I know you couldn't bear that.'

'Who'd protect the school and the Lost Rose if

Twinkle disappeared off on holiday?' said Mr Hart, laughing.

For those of you who remember, Story-seeker, the Lost Rose was an enormous ruby, which the girls had discovered on one of their many adventures at L'Etoile!

'Woof!' Twinkle barked as if to inform everyone she took her role as guardian of the Lost Rose very seriously and had no intention of leaving – even to be with her best girls.

'How have things been here?' asked Pippa, coming to join them. 'Have we missed anything exciting?'

'Oh hi, Pippa. Hi, Sally. I didn't see you both there. How many more of you are in that car? Did you all come together?' Mr Hart said, always amused by how the girls seemed to live in each other's pockets whether at school or away from it.

'We've been at Molly and Maria's house in the country this week, behaving perfectly. No mischief at all,' said Pippa, looking as innocent as she could.

'Woof!' Twinkle barked again, remembering the summer she'd spent with the girls at the Fitzfoster family house on the coast.

'Ha! Isn't she hilarious? She understands every

word we say. I'm sure she was remembering the time we single-handedly took on those smugglers at Wilton house,' said Molly.

'Not quite single-handedly, eh Twinkle?' Maria said, patting Twinkle's head. 'You're right, we couldn't have done it without you!'

'So what's Madame got up her sleeve for us this term, Mr Hart?' Molly asked.

'Ooh, yes! Tell us, Mr Hart,' Pippa begged.

'I could tell you, girls, but these fellas would have to cart you off to prison before you could spread any gossip!' Mr Hart said, nodding in the direction of not one, not two, but twelve stocky security guards wearing dark glasses.

'Wowsers!' Sally said. 'They look serious.'

'Not half,' Maria said, watching them curiously.

'Oh pleeeease, Mr H, you can't leave us in suspense. ICBI!' Molly groaned.'

(ICBI = I can't bear it, Story-seeker)

'Woof, woof!' Twinkle raced over to the girls' suitcases, lying in a heap on the drive.

'OK, OK, Twinks. You're quite right. We'd best go to Garland and unpack. In fact – why don't you come with us?' Maria said, looking at Mr Hart for approval. 'Pleeeease?'

'Sure,' he said, knowing it was always the easier option to give the girls exactly what they wanted. 'It's not as though I need to worry about her spilling the beans!'

'Woof, woof, woof!' Twinkle barked.

'Ha! I wouldn't be so sure, Mr H,' Sally said. 'We'll make a double agent out of you yet, Twinkle!'

'Bring her down when you go for supper will you, and I'll collect her then. Don't take her in the dining room with you though, or Mrs Mackle will throw a pink fit!' Mr Hart said.

'See you later then. Come on, Twinks,' said Molly, gathering up her bags. And with that, four girls and one very happy little black dog disappeared off up the path to Garland House.

'I can't believe Danya and Honey aren't here yet!' Molly said, desperate to see her friends.

Danya and Honey Sawyer were twins. Yes, you heard right, Story-seeker: another set of twins and since they'd met our girls and formed a gang of six, they'd been

inseparable – well, almost inseparable. Their mum and
dad, who were expecting a new baby any minute, had
taken their girls off to Disney World in Florida as a
surprise before their new brother or sister arrived.

'You'd have thought they'd have Skyped us at least
once while they were away, wouldn't you?' Maria
said, feeling a bit miffed that her partner in crime,
Danya, hadn't been in touch except for a couple of
texts promising to Skype soon.

'Oh, you know what Disney's like,' Sally said. 'It's
manic from start to finish.'

'I don't,' Pippa said.

'Don't what?' Sally asked.

'I don't know what Disney's like. I've never been.
I've seen it on the telly and read about it, but I've never
actually been,' Pippa said. 'Is it brilliant fun?'

Sally, Molly and Maria immediately felt very silly.
Sally had been lucky enough to go lots of times in the
dark years of living with the wicked Lucinda Marciano
and her famous film-star family in Los Angeles.

We say wicked, Story-seeker, as the Marcianos really had
made Sally's life a misery while she and her mum lived
and worked for them all those years. In fact the only good

♥ 5 ♥

thing they did was to bring her to L'Etoile as Lucinda's chaperone in the first year. Without that, she would never have met the best friends a girl could ask for.

The twins had been more times than they could remember, due to the fact that their dad, Brian Fitzfoster, was an even bigger kid at heart than his girls and couldn't resist a Disney day out.

'Oh Pips, you'd love it. In fact I've never met a more life-like Disney princess than you – with the voice too!' Molly said, not sure whether she was making things better or worse.

'We'll go! I'll ask Dad when his next trip to America is and if it's in the school holidays, we'll see if we can tag along for a week,' Maria said.

'Ooooooooh really?' said Pippa, her eyes shining. She loved these girls.

'Yes, really!' Molly and Maria exclaimed, watching as Twinkle jumped into Pippa's lap for a cuddle.

'I hope we're invited!' came two familiar voices as the door swung open and Danya and Honey's faces appeared.

'Danya! Honey!' Molly said, launching herself at Honey for a cuddle.

'Oh wow – you're wearing the latest Converse boots,

Honey. They are TDF!' Molly said, green with envy as she caught sight of Honey's feet.

 (TDF= to die for, Story-seeker)

'Trust you to have found a pair of the white leather ones; I've tried so many times to order them but they're sold out everywhere!'

'Good job we cleared out the Florida Mall then, isn't it?' Danya announced, walking in carrying a tower of shoeboxes. 'Converse for everyone!' she cried, as the boxes went crashing to the floor.

'No way!'

'Genius!'

'How did you even know our sizes?!'

'Oh thank you, girls. They're sooooo cool!' Molly said, admiring her feet. They were exactly the ones she'd been longing for since seeing them in her fashion magazine. 'GMTA!' !

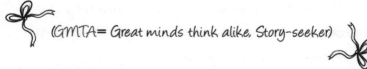 (GMTA= Great minds think alike, Story-seeker)

'Anything's possible if you have *twin radar*!' Danya said, giggling.

'Quick, you'd best lock the door again, in case

Miss Coates pops her head in. We've managed to get away with keeping our breaking and entering a secret for the past two terms – would be such a shame to give the game away now,' Maria said.

At the start of the new school year, there hadn't been a room big enough to house all six of our girls, Story-seeker, so after a torrent of pleading, Miss Coates had finally agreed to the next best thing, which was that the Sawyers would occupy the room next door to Molly, Maria, Pippa and Sally. The girls were thrilled as the rooms had an internal adjoining door. However, Miss Coates had explained that this door would remain padlocked at all times to prevent any midnight comings and goings. It will come as no big surprise, Story-seeker, that our two clever clogs Maria and Danya took one look at the padlock with the four-digit locking code and immediately set about trying to crack it. How hard could it be? Within fifteen minutes, Danya had managed to hack into the L'Etoile staff database and had written down any numbers Miss Coates might have chosen. Their first attempt was trying the day and month Miss Coates was born, 12 October – so 1210 – which failed. But their second attempt, the year she was born – 1974 – worked and the door had remained under their control ever since. What clever, sneaky girls!

'I nearly forgot,' Danya said, clicking the lock and spinning the digits.

'So what's new, gang?' Honey said, sitting on the end of Molly's bed.

'Ooh, you first, please. We all know what we've been up to. But we've been desperate to hear your news!' said Molly. 'How was Mickey Mouse?'

'Amazing! Such fun! I don't think there was a ride we haven't been on – twice!' said Danya. 'Dad got us fast passes so we didn't even have to queue. It was soooo cool! We'll get them again when we go, Pippa!' she said, having overheard the girls' conversation as they'd arrived.

'I can't wait,' Pippa said, dreamily.

'Let's see, what happened, Danya?' Honey paused. 'It goes without saying how much we missed you, but things just got so busy!'

'Too busy to answer a Skype call?' Maria said, looking slightly hurt.

'Sorry about that, Maria. A new baby sends everything into chaos!' Danya said, pausing for the others to catch on.

'What? Your mum's had the baby?'

'Yes!' Honey said. 'A girl! A beautiful sister. Can you believe it?'

'Oh my goodness, congratulations. What's her name?' Molly said.

'Flori. Obviously . . . given her surprise arrival in Florida! Still, could have been worse – could have been Minnie or Goofy or something.'

The girls descended into fits of giggles.

'And is your mum OK? When did it happen?' Sally asked.

'We'd only just got to the hotel from the plane when Mum started having tummy pains and next thing we knew, she and Dad were whisked off to hospital and we were being summoned to come and visit our little sister,' Honey said.

'Ah, so cute. Do you just love her? I can't wait to see her. Do you think your mum might let us have a cuddle at some point?' Pippa said.

'Woof!' Twinkle barked, her nose appearing from under Maria's bed. Hearing her favourite word, *cuddle*, she leapt onto Pippa's bed.

'Twinkle!' Honey and Danya said together. 'Where did you spring from?'

'She's been so quiet I forgot she was here,' Molly said, smiling as the Sawyers showered the little black dog with affection.

'What were you going to say about when we can

meet Flori?' Pippa asked.

'Sorry, yes – cuddles! Definitely. Mum's going to bring her down to L'Etoile at the end of term to meet you all,' Danya said.

'We've got to send her a pressie. Some sort of tutu and tiara I think!' Molly said, reaching for her laptop.

'Molly, it's just as well Mum and Dad didn't have any more children. If we had a little brother or sister, they'd be doomed to life as your doll!' said Maria.

'I never thought of that!' said Honey, thinking about the fancy-dress outfits she could get her in.

'Ah, we're all so happy Flori's here. Even if she did scream the plane down all the way home! To be honest, I'm pleased to be back at school for a good night's sleep,' Danya said with a yawn.

'Can't guarantee that,' Maria said, hoping for a sleepless night of L'Etoile adventure soon.

'Ooh, yes please!' Danya answered. 'I don't mind *that* sort of exhaustion!'

As the girls continued to chat and unpack, they suddenly became aware of something going on outside. Twinkle was the first with her nose against the glass.

'What's going on?' Pippa said, racing Sally to the window.

'Woof woof!' Twinkle said, pawing at the pane.

'Um, girls, I think we'd better go take a look. Something or rather someone is definitely happening out there!' Sally said excitedly.

All six girls huddled at the window, but nothing could have prepared them for the spectacle unfolding outside.

'Sorry Twinkle, but I think you'd better stay here for a moment, or we might lose you,' Molly said.

'We won't be long. You can sit on my bed . . . as a treat!' said Maria.

2

Now That's What I Call an Entrance!

*I*t wasn't long before the entire third year found themselves among the rest of school outside.

'Who do you think it is?' Belle squealed, scrambling through crowds of excited L'Etoilettes and staff.

'It's got to be someone pretty special to warrant all this security,' Amanda said.

'Imagine if it's a pop star!' Alice answered.

'What, to sing us into the summer term?' Nancy joked. 'Here's hoping!'

'I saw a motorcade like that go past us in London once and it turned out to be the queen on her way to Windsor Castle!' said Betsy.

'The queen?' Sofia and Daisy gasped. 'Oh my gosh. How cool would that be . . . a visit from the queen!'

Molly suddenly had a thought . . . the sort of thought that *Molly dreams* were made of.

 What if it was Prince Henry, heir to the throne of England, coming back to collect her and whisk her off to the palace to become his princess? What if, indeed . . . Story-seeker!

Maria and Danya were the only two girls who watched in silence as the never-ending motorcade of sleek, black cars snaked its way down the long drive.

'What do you think, Dan?' Maria whispered.

'Not sure – but I don't think they're British. Check out those little tricolour flags on the middle car. They're not Union Jacks, that's for sure,' Danya answered, craning her neck for a better view.

'Well spotted!' Maria said, impressed. She hadn't noticed the flags but now that she looked, something in her extraordinary memory rang a bell. 'I know what country they're from . . . saffron, green and white with a blue wheel in the centre, right?'

'I'd have said orange – but if you prefer saffron then, yep! Can't make out a blue wheel from here though! How can you see that?' Danya asked.

'I can't, but there's something in the middle which makes me think it might be that. I was flicking through a book on flags only the other day in Dad's study and remember seeing that very one!' Maria said.

'Flicking through a book of flags . . . as only *you* would!' Danya teased.

'I know, I know – I'm the world's least-known super-geek!'

'Second only to me!' replied Danya.

'She's a princess . . . ' Pippa said, panting from fighting her way through the excitable crowd. 'From India . . . an Indian princess!'

'How did you . . . ?' Maria said, annoyed to have been pipped to the post.

'How do you know that?' Molly and Honey asked in unison.

'Blimey, Pips. Maria and I thought we were good – but you've just scooped the prize for super-geek!' Danya said.

'Eh?' Pippa looked confused.

'She's right. I heard it too! A real princess from India,' Sally said, appearing from behind Pippa.

'The Indian national flag. Saffron, green and white

with a blue wheel in the middle. I told you, didn't I?'
Maria said to Danya.

Maria Fitzfoster has a track record of always being right, Story-seeker!

At this point everyone had fallen silent and was listening intently to Pippa and Sally.

'Sal – are you stalking me? I didn't realise you were even with me!' Pippa asked in surprise.

'I only came after you because you dropped this when you ran off,' Sally said, pulling out a little purple notebook of what looked like handwritten poetry.

'My lyric book!' Pippa exclaimed. 'Oh thank goodness for you, Sally. I would never have been able to replace that. I hadn't even noticed it was missing! I was supposed to post it to Mr Fuller before the end of the holidays so he could work on this new track, but I hadn't quite finished the last one, so as soon as I saw Mrs Fuller on the steps, I figured I'd give it to her – that's when I overheard Mr Hart ask her whether he should start taking the princess's luggage to her room, or whether he should just leave it to her security. I came straight back to tell you all!'

'Oh my gosh! A real-life princess!' Molly was

practically dribbling. 'Staying here, at my school! Wouldn't that be OOTW!'

(OOTW = Out of this world, Story-seeker)

The news went round like wildfire.

'A princess!'

'From India. How exotic!'

'Do you think she'll be in our year?'

'Should we courtsey?'

'Will we be allowed to talk to her?'

'Imagine her wardrobe!'

'I hope she's nice!'

'Hold the front page! Check out old Ruby! She's outdone herself this time!' Maria said, spotting their headmistress making her own entrance on the front steps of L'Etoile, draped in a beautiful burnt-orange silk sari.

'OK – so the lippy clashes – but I LOVE the orange. She's a one-woman sunset!' Molly said to Fashion Faye who was standing on her left, taking photos on her phone.

'Agreed! Absolutely divine!' Faye said, already thinking about how to incorporate an Indian theme into her new designs. *Wonderful colours*, she thought.

Suddenly, Madame Ruby raised her right arm and, as if by magic, the crowd fell silent, just as the main car with the flags drew up beside her. Everyone was holding their breath, desperate for their first glimpse of the princess.

Security guards scurried around, checking for goodness knows what. The driver of the lead car got out and moved to open the rear passenger door. A gasp went up as one bejewelled foot stepped daintily onto the drive, quickly followed by the most immaculate human being anyone had ever seen.

'I think someone's just stolen your Disney princess crown, Pips!' Molly whispered, as her eyes followed the most beautiful dark-haired girl she'd ever seen.

'Yup!' Pippa said, watching wide-eyed. What was it about this girl that just exuded . . . well . . . royalty?

The princess stood deadly still, as though waiting for something to give her the go-ahead. Ah, that was it. The driver ran around the car to open the other passenger door, and out stepped a short, very smartly dressed Indian lady, carrying a briefcase in one hand, and a pair of gloves in the other.

The welcoming committee was immediately on the move.

'Here she goes,' Maria muttered under her breath,

as Madame Ruby glided down the stone steps as though they were a red carpet. You could have heard a pin drop as everyone waited for the princess to speak.

'Welcome to L'Etoile, Your Royal Highness,' Madame Ruby said, lowering her gaze.

The princess smiled sweetly and nodded. Then Madame Ruby turned to the other lady. 'And to you, Your Excellency. Thank you so much for coming.'

'Who's *Your Excellency*, d'you reckon?' Danya whispered to Maria. 'Don't tell me, you've just been flicking through a book on how to address a VIP?'

Maria gave her a friendly elbow. 'As a matter of fact . . . ' she paused. 'Just kidding. The only person I've ever heard addressed as *Your Excellency* was when Dad introduced us to the French ambassador at the Royal Ballet last Christmas, so if I had to guess, I'd go for the Indian ambassador.'

'No way!' Danya said. 'If you've got that right, I'll do your homework for the rest of the year!'

'If I've got that right, I'll be better off doing my own homework, thank you!' Maria grinned.

'Shh!' Honey whispered, desperate to hear every word. So far, Madame Ruby had introduced Mrs Fuller and some of the other teachers and everyone was busy bowing so as not to commit any royal etiquette crime.

'Do you think Ruby's going to introduce her to us now? Or wait until tomorrow's assembly?' Pippa said.

'Not sure. But she's a clever old boot. By keeping this whole thing a big secret, she made sure we were all so curious we came scurrying out to put on a good welcome show for the princess's arrival. I bet she can't believe her luck. The atmosphere is electric out here!' Danya answered.

'Will you lot *shh*! Some of us are trying to hear!' Molly exploded and then immediately ducked behind Daisy to avoid the glare of Mr Potts, the music teacher, who was standing close by.

'Girls . . . ' Madame Ruby exclaimed in her poshest voice.

'Here she goes . . .' said Maria, secretly pleased they would at last have official word on what was going on.

'Staff and students of L'Etoile, School for Stars. Please join me in welcoming Princess Ameera of India.' Madame Ruby paused as a gasp rippled around the crowd. 'I'm delighted to tell you that the princess will be staying with us until the end of term and I know you will all help me to make her time here memorable.' Everyone clapped and cheered as the princess simply smiled and nodded as if to thank them.

'Thank you, girls. Now I would like you all to return to your houses and continue with your new-term preparations.'

'For round two, no doubt,' Sally said, remembering how Madame Ruby loved the sound of her own voice in every first-term assembly. It was her show time, where she captivated her audience with tales of exciting times to come.

With that, Princess Ameera and the other lady –

for we don't yet know whether she was the Indian ambassador or not (although knowing Maria, Story-seeker, she probably was!)

– followed Madame Ruby through the big black L'Etoile doors, under that gold L'Etoile star, for the grand L'Etoile tour!'

3

An Unlikely Pair

'*I* bet she's looking at the Lost Rose ruby right now, thinking, I've got bigger gems than that in my jewellery box at home!' Molly said, imagining what it must be like to be a real princess.

'I know. Did you see how many suitcases came out of all those cars? Miss Coates will have had to give her an extra bedroom just as a walk-in wardrobe! I bet Mr Hart was glad the security guards carried them in. Imagine the dresses!' Honey said, suddenly.

'Imagine the shoes! IIH!' said Molly.

'IIH?' Honey said, convinced that she felt it too, if only she knew what that little Mollyism meant!

'IIH . . . I'm in heaven . . . duh!' Molly said, and

both girls sighed with happiness.

Maria and Danya rolled their eyes at their predictable sisters.

'How's all this going to work then?' Pippa asked. 'Do you think that she's really going to live at L'Etoile, with us, just with an entire security crack team following her every move?'

'Woof!' Twinkle barked.

'Oh, Twinks. If only you could talk. You could tell us what's happening, couldn't you?' Pippa said. 'I bet you know *everything*, don't you?'

'Woof, woof!'

'I don't think the bodyguards can follow her everywhere she goes. There has to be some kind of normality for her, don't you think?' Danya said.

'There does seem to be one main guy with her at all times. Did you see him . . . the really massive, slightly older one . . . you know, *Butch*?'

The girls giggled at Maria's nickname for Princess Ameera's head of security.

'You might be right there,' Danya said. 'The others seemed to be taking their orders from him.'

'Exactly!' Maria said. 'He's clearly the boss. The princess's driver didn't dare move until he got the nod from Butch to open her door.'

'I'm not sure this is all going to work out so well for
me!' Sally groaned suddenly. She'd been fairly quiet
since they got back to Garland.

'Why, Sally?' Molly asked in surprise. 'Whatever
do you mean?'

'You know what I'm like. I'm a clumsy goofball on
a good day. Just imagine what kind of state I'll get
myself into around a real-life princess. I'm going to be
a bag of nerves. I just hope she's not in our year! How
old do you think she is?'

'Darling Sally, don't be daft – you'll be fine! If
you think you're nervous, just imagine what's going
through her mind. We all know each other, but she's on
her own and that can't be much fun at all,' Molly said.

Sally nodded.

'I wouldn't worry about it. We probably won't
have anything to do with her anyway,' said Maria.
'Madame Ruby will keep as close to her as possible at
all times, and if her ambassador chaperone, Butch and
his bodyguard army are anything to go by, none of us
will come within a million miles of her.'

'I wouldn't be so sure about that,' Danya said, appearing through the connecting door, iPad in hand.

'Princess Ameera, daughter of Prince Imran and Princess Preeti. Born . . . wait for it . . . same year as us! She'll definitely be in some of our lessons – if not in our class!'

Sally was white as a sheet. 'I knew it. Just my luck.'

'What else does it say about her, Dan?' Molly asked.

Danya continued, scrolling. 'There's nothing here about any hobbies, if that's what you mean, but there is one interesting thing . . . It says she is an only child, adopted into the royal family by her parents, who were unable to have a child of their own.'

'Adopted! Oh my! It's like a fairy tale,' said Molly.

'Yes, yes! A real rags-to-riches story!' said Honey.

Sally immediately felt a little less daunted. Knowing that this princess had been catapulted into royal life through no fault of her own made her feel much better for some reason.

'Rags to riches? We don't know she was plucked from complete poverty. She might always have been destined to live a life of luxury,' Danya said.

Sally felt worse again.

'Well, whoever her biological parents were, it's quite a responsibility, becoming a princess,' Maria said.

'But if she was adopted as a baby, she won't know any different, will she?' Sally said.

'It's the nature-or-nurture question,' said Maria.

'What?' Molly said, never ceasing to be surprised by her sister's brainy moments.

'Nature or nurture. People who believe in nature say that you are born a certain way and no matter what influences you have in life you will always be that way. Nurture says it's what happens to you and how you are raised,' Maria said, realising she'd lost everyone but Danya by then.

'Whatever happened, she's Princess Ameera to us and I for one can't wait to be introduced.' Honey announced.

'Let's go to supper then. I imagine Mackle will have got the silver out for her first royal banquet!' Pippa said as her tummy rumbled loud enough for them all to hear.

'It's already gone six p.m. – we're late,' Sally said, glancing at the clock.

'Come on, Twinks! Mr Hart will be thinking we've dog-napped you!' Molly said, tying a scarf to the little black dog's collar as a lead.

And with that, the six forever friends raced off to the Ivy Room hoping to catch a glimpse of how a royal eats supper.

Having dropped Twinkle off, the twins, Pippa and Sally had to sneak in at the back door so as not to incur the wrath of any member of staff who might happen to be passing. How could they have been so late, today of all days? Too much chatting as always. But luckily for them, staff and students alike were too busy staring at the royal end of the room to notice.

The Ivy Room didn't have its usual 'feeding time at the zoo' atmosphere, mainly because everyone was too busy trying to make an impression rather than gossiping.

Usually, the teacher's dining tables were by the French doors, three tables in a line, so that the whole dining room could be easily observed. But this evening they'd been pushed together and covered in a crisp, white tablecloth and set as if for a feast.

'Can you believe it? Talk about pushing the boat out!' Pippa said, helping herself to a scoop of less-lumpy-than-normal mashed potato.

'The novelty is soon going to wear off for old Mackle if she's got to produce this sort of service every day.' Danya answered.

'Even the broccoli is green today, as opposed to its usual boiled-within-an-inch-of-its-life shade of sludge-brown!' Sally said.

'The longer this lasts the better,' Molly said, almost looking forward to eating her chicken Kiev.

'Perhaps we could have a word with Butch to tell old Mackle to keep up the good work,' Maria said, nodding in the direction of the XXL bodyguard standing at the end of the room.

'Ha! Excellent. I could see those two as a couple!' Pippa giggled. 'But there'd be no dinner left for the rest of us!'

'Pippa!' Honey and Danya said before bursting out laughing.

As the girls tucked in to their supper, conversations bounced between the new princess and what they'd been up to that summer. Sally was bubbling with excitement as she told the girls all about how she and her mum had spent a couple of weeks with family in Ireland, the highlight of which was that she'd learned to ride. She had the girls in stitches, demonstrating her galloping technique, and was in full flow when she suddenly noticed her friends' faces fall.

'What's up? Have I got ketchup on my chops or something?' she asked, quickly wiping her mouth on her sleeve.

The girls shook their heads but it was too late. They just had to sit and watch whatever it was that was coming.

Suddenly Sally felt a hand lightly tap her left shoulder, making her jump out of her skin. She swung around. 'Madame Ruby!' she gasped. *I knew I should have saved that horsey story until after lights out. How could I have been so stupid? I'm for it now!*

'Sally. Apologies for interrupting your rather animated equestrian tale but I wondered if I might borrow you for a moment,' the headmistress said, giving the others an *I hope you are behaving yourselves, L'Etoilettes*, look.

'Me?' Sally said. 'Um ... yes ... of course.' Dutifully she followed the headmistress over to the royal table.

Her heart was thumping so loudly, she was worried she might not hear anything anyone might say to her. *Get a grip, Sal, get a grip!* she told herself over and over.

'Princess Ameera ... may I introduce you to Miss Sally Sudbury, another of our students who joined us from abroad, only to make L'Etoile her home,' Madame Ruby said, beckoning to Sally to step forward.

So that's why she picked me. What do I do now, shake her hand? Smile and do nothing? Courtsey? She settled on a courtsey, hoping for the best.

'It's a pleasure to meet you, Miss Sudbury,' Princess Ameera said sweetly. 'Do sit down.' She pointed to the empty seat opposite.

As Sally walked around the table, she was only too aware that every single pair of eyes in that dining room was on her. *Don't trip, don't trip! Phew! Made it.*

'Sally joined us from Los Angeles in the first year and, I'm delighted to say, has been with us ever since. In fact I think I'm right in saying your family has since moved to England permanently as a result?' Madame Ruby continued.

'Yes,' Sally said. *Just keep it simple, Sal.*

'So you'll know all about moving to a foreign country and the best way to make it feel like home?' Madame Ruby said.

'Um, yes, I think so,' Sally said, racking her brains.

'Wonderful!' said the short Indian lady who'd arrived with Princess Ameera. 'I am Mrs Kapoor, the Indian ambassador, and while I have had the honour of accompanying the princess to L'Etoile today, it is not possible for me to remain here for the duration of her stay. Hence I asked Madame Ruby if there was someone she could assign to the princess as a companion. Someone reliable. Does that sound like something you'd be able to do efficiently, Miss Sudbury?'

'Me?' Sally said, incredulous. *They've chosen me?*

'It would be my pleasure,' she said, daring to look the princess in the eye. 'If you're sure.'

Princess Ameera nodded.

It's quite amazing what someone having a little confidence in you does for your own confidence, Story-seeker. Talk about a boost!!

'That's settled then,' Madame Ruby said. 'Princess Ameera is to be in Three Alpha with you, Sally, and I would like you to help her in any way you can. Try to think back to those early days at L'Etoile when you didn't know where anything was, or indeed who anyone was. Your guidance and friendship will be invaluable to the princess and in return your life will be enriched by this whole experience.'

Goodness me. Wait until the others get a load of this!

'I'd . . . I mean . . . I would be honoured, Madame Ruby,' Sally said, blushing. *Was this really happening?*

Princess Ameera turned to Sally. 'Perhaps you would be kind enough to collect me on your way to assembly in the morning? Even though Madame Ruby gave us a most thorough tour of L'Etoile this afternoon, I'm not sure I'll remember where everything is straight away.'

'Of course I will,' said Sally, brimming with pride. 'In fact, I'll be going back to my room this evening. Would you like me to come and show you where it is in relation to you, so you know where I am in case you need anything? I could also introduce you to some of the other girls in Three Alpha, so it won't feel quite so strange in the morning,' Sally said, trying to think what she would want if she was in the princess's shoes.

'Oh I think that might be a bit too much this eve—' Mrs Kapoor started, but was immediately interrupted.

'That's a lovely idea. Thank you, Sally. Could you come and get me in about half an hour?'

Sally nodded.

Madame Ruby and Mrs Fuller exchanged knowing glances, not entirely sure that being introduced to Sally's mischievous friends was quite the start they wanted for Princess Ameera, but it couldn't be avoided for ever. They would be in the same class after all.

'That's settled then. Thank you, Sally. You are excused,' Madame Ruby said, secretly proud of how Sally had risen to the occasion.

'Thank you,' said Sally, and with a few nods and another dodgy courtsey, she left the now very empty dining room and made her way through the gossip mill that was Garland House. She couldn't wait to get to her girls. They must be desperate to hear her news.

4

A Royal Conundrum

Danya and Honey hadn't even bothered going to their bedroom and were sitting on Molly's bed with the others, impatiently waiting for Sally's return.'

'I wonder why old Ruby asked Sally,' Honey said. 'Not that I'm jealous or anything . . . '

Danya gave her a sideways glance.

'Well, maybe just a little.' Honey couldn't hide anything from her sister.

'I'm just pleased it was one of us . . . when you think they could have picked anyone. At least this way we're that bit closer to an introduction!' Molly said, unsure why she felt the need to reapply her lip-gloss before bed.

'I'm ba-ack!' Sally said, bursting through the door.

'We're dying to know what's happened. Quick! Tell us everything! Don't leave a thing out . . . ' Molly said, scarcely drawing a breath. 'Was she nice? What did she say? I'm so pleased they picked you. I mean, WATC it would be one of us! What did you say? What did she smell like?'

(WATC = What are the chances, Story-seeker)

'Molly! Let poor Sally get a word in,' Maria said. 'Or you'll never find out anything!'

 If there was anything Maria hated, it was uncontrollable hysteria, Story-seeker. If only everyone was a little less hysterical, things would get done a whole lot quicker!

'What did she smell like?' Pippa asked Molly, a bit confused why that was relevant. 'Is that a serious question?'

Sally was on cloud nine. She'd never felt so important. Not even when she'd been elected as the auctioneer at the charity auction the girls had hosted when they were second years.

'Sally! Sit!' Molly instructed as if she was talking to Twinkle.

Sally immediately sat on the end of her bed and took a deep breath.

'OK! I hear you. But, before I start, can I just ask . . . did I look like a complete doughnut when I courtsied? I had no idea what I was supposed to do. My head was swimming,' Sally said, her cheeks flushing red.

'Oh, darling, you did brilliantly. No girl in that room wanted to be in your shoes,' Pippa said. 'I mean, plucking you from your supper like that in front of everyone, with no warning. No one would have wanted that!'

'Well, except maybe Honey,' Danya giggled.

'Or Miss Molly!' Maria laughed.

'Hey!' Molly said.

'They're right though, aren't they?' Honey said, unashamedly. 'We'd have both jumped at the chance to be the first to meet the princess!'

'But I didn't know it was to meet the princess when I felt that tap on my shoulder, did I? I nearly fainted when I saw Madame Ruby standing there. I thought that was it. That my time was up and I was about to be expelled or something for doing my *horsing* around in the dining room,' Sally said.

'I know. I don't know how you held it together. You should have seen the look on your face when you saw old Ruby,' Pippa said, thinking how nervous she would have felt.

'And you should have seen yours!' said Sally. She'd never forget the wild panic in the girls' eyes when they'd spotted Madame Ruby making a beeline for her.

'You must have been so nervous when you actually met the princess,' Honey said.

'I was. My butterflies had butterflies! But I didn't need to be. Princess Ameera was so sweet. I mean, really lovely. Her skin almost glows up close.'

'Was she really?' Molly said. 'Perfect skin? Perfect nails? Perfect hair?'

'Perfect perfection!' Sally answered. 'And the best news of all is that she's going to be in our class!'

'What?'

'Really?'

'WATC?'

'Yes, and old Ruby wants *me* to show her the ropes. How did she put it? Yes, that was it: she asked me if I'd be her *companion* for the duration of her stay, as the princess doesn't know where anything is or have any friends yet.'

'Wow, that's so cool!' Pippa said.

'I know! I think they picked me because I moved over here from abroad so they think I can help her deal with being homesick or something . . . not that I ever was homesick for Lucifette and the Marcianos – although I did miss Mum a lot . . . ' said Sally, getting sidetracked.

'Sally! That's so wonderful. You're simply the best person for the job. CAAC! You won't be in her face, asking too many questions or anything. I'm so happy for you,' Molly said, knowing full well she'd have bombarded the princess with questions from morning till night.

(CAAC = Cool as a cucumber, Story-seeker.)

'Ah, thanks, girls. I don't think anything this exciting has ever happened to me,' Sally said and then a look of panic came across her face. 'What time is it? I said I'd pick her up in thirty minutes . . . how long have I been back here?'

'About half an hour,' Danya said, looking at her watch.

'Pick the princess up? For what?' Molly said, jumping up as if she'd just been stung by something.

'To bring her to meet you all, of course!' Sally grinned.

'What?' the girls shrieked.

'What, right now? Right, right now?' Honey asked, relieved she wouldn't be visiting *their* room. It was nowhere near tidy enough for visitors . . . especially ones with tiaras!

'Right now,' Sally said, making for the door. 'She's in the room I used to share with Lucifette at the other end of the corridor. And she's waiting for me so I'd best get down there!'

'OMG, OMG, OMG, sugar, sugar, sugar!' Molly said, beside herself with excitement.

'I know and look at this place! Quick! We need to clear up!' Pippa said, but Danya and Maria were way ahead of her.

Clothes were being flung around the room as if they were in a massive tumble dryer.
It's quite incredible how quickly you can surface-clean in under a minute, Story-seeker. You just have to hope no one opens a cupboard or looks under a bed!

Knock, knock.

'Shh . . . shhhhh . . . she's here . . . ' Honey whispered as the door opened.

Princess Ameera stood in the doorway of the girls' bedroom, as beautiful as the first time she had stepped out of the car, only this time in a simple blue silk dress and ballet-pink pumps.

Molly, Maria, Danya, Honey and Pippa stood in a line to welcome her.

'Princess Ameera, these are my friends: Molly and Maria Fitzfoster, Honey and Danya Sawyer and Pippa Burrows . . . ' Sally said, extending her arm to the five girls bobbing up and down.

The princess smiled. 'It's a pleasure to meet you. But please, call me Ameera.'

'Ooh I couldn't possibly, Princess,' Molly said. 'It just wouldn't be right. I'm Molly . . . and I love your dress!'

'Why, thank you,' Ameera said, thinking how funny it was that this girl should like her leisurewear. 'I very much like your top.'

Molly was beside herself with glee. She knew this would be just the thing for a royal introduction and had been right on the fashion money!

'And I'm Maria . . . Am-eera,' Maria said, proud to be the first to use her Christian name.

And as the others introduced themselves the intensity levels in the room began to drop and they started to relax a bit. Who'd have thought when they left for school that morning that they'd now be sitting on beds, drinking beakers of Maggie Sudbury's homemade pink lemonade with a real-life princess!

'So . . . Your Highness—' Honey began.

'Ameera, please,' the princess responded quickly.

'Ameera, then. What made you decide to come to L'Etoile?'

'It was actually my idea following something I read. I have the most wonderful life in India, but it feels so cocooned. The internet is brilliant but it makes me realise that there's a whole world that I know nothing about.'

'Don't you just love the internet?' Danya said, not noticing Honey roll her eyes. Of all the questions you could ask your first royal and Danya chose the internet!

'I don't know where I'd be without it!' said Ameera. 'It's opened up my eyes to many things. Take L'Etoile, for example. I can remember Googling famous English legends last year and an article popped up about hidden treasure being discovered at this very school. Madame Ruby showed it to us today – the ruby . . . Lost Rose—'

'That was us!' Maria said excitedly and then remembered herself. 'I'm so sorry. I didn't mean to interrupt.'

'No, please! This is amazing. You were the girls who discovered and solved the mystery? How lucky I am to meet you!' Ameera said, her eyes flashing. 'After reading about it, sometimes I used to pretend that there was treasure hidden at home in the palace and I would go on a quest to find it.'

'I should imagine your palace is full of treasures, far more exciting and valuable than our Lost Rose,' said Maria.

'Yes, yes of course. It's full of beautiful things. But no hidden treasures. And besides, adventures aren't fun when you're having them alone. I can't imagine the fun you had solving that mystery together,' Ameera said. 'You'll have to tell me the whole story some time, from start to finish.'

'Absolutely,' Pippa said, only too familiar with what it was like to be an only child. 'And you must tell us what you like doing. There might be something we can do together.'

'I'd like that very much,' Ameera said, sincerely. 'Now please, tell me all about your experience of life here at L'Etoile. Do you like it here?'

The girls smiled. No one could love anything more!

'Where should we start?' Sally said and the girls, now so much more relaxed, busied about giving the princess as much gossip on students, staff and dog as quickly as possible.

' . . . so when Mrs Butter – or old *Butterboots* as we call her, mentions her ancestors might be linked to the British royal family, for heaven's sake don't ask any questions, or you'll be there until your eighteenth birthday!'

Ameera chuckled. 'That's so funny. I'm never going to remember all this when I meet people tomorrow. You're going to have to take it in turns to whisper who did what whenever we meet someone. I'm awfully glad Miss Marciano is no longer with us. She sounds like a complete nightmare!'

'And you only know the half of it! We'd need a week to fill you in on that horror story!' Sally said.

'I look forward to it. Your student blogger has been giving me an overview of L'Etoile for the past couple of weeks. Tell me, girls. What's the gossip on *Yours, L'Etoilette*? Do you think she really is a student or do you think it's a teacher's way of keeping an eye on the girls?'

Maria's mouth dropped to the floor in surprise. *Yours, L'Etoilette?* she thought. *But that's impossible!*

Only Honey (who didn't know who the real *Yours, L'Etoilette* was either) responded. 'I'm pretty sure it's one of the girls. I never really suspected anything else, nor have I ever needed to go to her for advice.'

'I only ask because I found her a bit intimidating,' said Ameera.

'Intimidating?' said Danya (who also hadn't been let into Maria's little secret yet).

'Why exactly?' Maria asked stonily.

'It was all the questions she asked. When I'd be arriving, who would be accompanying me, how much freedom I'd have to take part in student activities, and the list goes on.'

The girls were silent.

'I mean, having thought I'd made the best decision in the world to come here, I was a bit worried. The last email she sent me, she even suggested I get up to mischief to try to fit in with the girls in my year. Can you imagine how much trouble I'd be in?' Ameera said.

Seeing the look of anger on Maria's face, Pippa jumped in with a question. 'How did you come to be in contact with her in the first place?'

'She . . . she emailed me. I guessed Madame Ruby put us in touch with each other, thinking it might be a good way to introduce me to the world of L'Etoile,' Ameera said.

'And you're sure it was *Yours, L'Etoilette*?' Maria asked, trying her best to act normally.

'Yes! Why, do you know who she is?' Ameera said.

'Um . . . ' Maria stumbled.

'No one knows,' Danya jumped in quickly, realising something was up.

'No. I've never emailed her but I know lots of people who do and everyone says she's really helpful,' Honey said innocently.

Suddenly there was a knock at the door and the housemistress, Miss Coates, appeared at the door.

'Sorry to disturb you, but it's time for lights out.'

Saved by the bell, Maria thought.

'Good night, everyone. Thank you again for being so welcoming. I look forward to seeing you in the morning,' Ameera said, standing up to leave.

'Good night, Princess,' Molly said, not being able to help herself.

And with that Princess Ameera left with Miss Coates for her first night in her new school.

'What the heck?' Maria exploded in as much of a whisper as she could manage.

'Mimi, calm down,' Molly said.

'Something you want to tell us, Maria?' Danya said. 'Or should I call you *Yours, L'Etoilette*?'

'What?' Honey said in surprise, the only girl in the room not to have been told, or worked out, Maria's secret. 'You're *Yours, L'Etoilette*?'

Maria nodded.

'Why didn't you tell us before?' Honey said, feeling rather left out.

'There wasn't really a need to. Had you guys ever tried to email *Yours, L'Etoilette* for advice, I definitely would have come clean, but you never have, so it's just never come up,' Maria said.

'I don't know why we're so surprised. Who else could pull off this split personality so successfully?' Danya said, full of admiration. 'So what's the story with the princess? I'm sensing you don't know anything about any email correspondence with her?'

'You sense right. I'm incensed!' Maria exclaimed. 'I've been hacked. I must have been!' she said, logging in to her *Yours, L'Etoilette* account. 'I haven't logged in since last term. I never use it over the holidays. Let's see – yes, here – my last conversation was with

Fashion Faye when she was overloaded at the end of last term and needed some scheduling advice to get all the costumes done on time.'

'And there's nothing after that?' Pippa said, peering over Maria's shoulder.

'No. Look . . . nothing.'

'I just don't get it!' Molly exclaimed.

'One thing's for sure: the faker has to be someone at L'Etoile. No one outside the school would even know *Yours, L'Etoilette* exists,' Maria said.

'Unless they'd been told about her!' Sally said.

'True, but who would do such a thing?' Honey said. 'Especially to give the princess bad advice! I mean, telling her to get herself into trouble of all things. Where do they think we are, St Trinian's?'

'Ooh, I would love to have been a St Trinian!' Molly said, smiling at the thought.

'Don't get sidetracked, Moll! This is serious!' snapped Maria.

'Me too,' Honey winked at Molly.

'You said it's someone at the school, but no one except Madame Ruby and probably Mrs Fuller knew the princess was even coming and neither of them would have wanted to scupper her arrival,' Pippa said.

Maria was stumped. None of it made sense — the

why, the who, or the how – and that didn't please her at all.

'Wait . . . I've got an idea . . . check your deleted items,' Danya said. 'If they have been in your account deleting emails as they go so you didn't see them, they might have forgotten to empty the trash.'

Maria didn't know what she'd prefer: to find out that she, Maria Fitzfoster, had been hacked by someone of equal intelligence – if that was the case, at least she might be able to see what had been written – *or* to find out her email account had been hacked by someone of superior intelligence, so that she didn't have a clue what the conversations had been.

'Argh! Spinny ball drives me crazy!' Pippa said as they watched the little multi coloured ball going around and around on the screen as they waited for the trash to load.

'There!' Danya shrieked as about ten deleted emails popped up between Maria (supposedly) and ameera@secureroyalnetwork.co.in

'I can't believe it! How could I not have noticed?' Maria said, annoyed beyond belief.

'If you haven't logged in since last term you couldn't possibly have known,' Danya said.

Silently the girls crowded around the screen,

reading email after email between a nervous princess about to join a new school in a new country and a very unsympathetic *Yours, L'Etoilette*.

'It's a wonder she ended up coming here at all,' Molly said.

'What are we going to do? It's not even like we can report it without giving the game away that you're *Yours*,' Molly said.

'You could just try changing the password and putting some more security on the account. I've downloaded this supposedly bulletproof anti-hacking software. Want to give that a go?' Danya suggested.

'I'm not sure. Aren't we better pretending we haven't noticed so we can keep an eye on the conversations – if there are any more?' Maria said. 'Even though we've no idea who the faker is, or why they're doing it, at least we know something that's not quite right is going on. But they don't know *we know*, so we're a step ahead there.'

'Yes, I'm with you, Maria. You think they haven't finished with their meddling then?' Danya asked.

'I don't know. Depends what their intention is. *Yours* was set up as an advice blog, and while the advice the faker's given so far is pretty hideous, what's clear from Ameera's emails is that she's opening up more and more,' Maria said.

'Gosh, how awful. She must be so desperate to talk to someone – anyone – about her thoughts and worries, she's even prepared to share with this vile faker,' Sally said, remembering what it was like to feel alone in a crowd. Even though she had been surrounded by people when she lived with the Marciano family in Hollywood, she never had anyone to talk to or share things with – apart from her mum, who was always working – and it seemed Princess Ameera was the same.

Who'd have thought Sally Sudbury would have so much in common with a real-life princess, Story-seeker? It just goes to show that everyone has the same worries, no matter what their situation, and that there's nothing as important as friendship.

'How about if you start writing some messages of your own? More welcoming ones, just as you would have if none of this had happened and the princess emailed *Yours* for advice. The faker will know that as soon as the term starts, there's a chance the real *Yours* will be back online to help her fellow students. Even if the faker logs on and sees you're already communicating with Ameera, it won't stop them from meddling. They can continue to send and delete messages thinking we still have no idea. At least this way we can see everything and can try to find out what's going on,' said Danya.

'Yes, that would work. And I don't think we should say anything to Ameera yet. We're not even into the term yet and we've uncovered the beginnings of a mystery – I for one don't want to worry the princess until we've got to the bottom of it. I wonder what it's all about,' Maria said, thoughtfully.

'I don't know, but I don't like it and that poor girl is going to need our help,' Molly said firmly.

'It would be rude not to. After all, mystery is our middle name!' Sally cried.

And with that, six tired and confused young ladies went to bed. What an eventful start to the term!

5

Introductions

Sally couldn't help but feel rather royal herself as she escorted her new friend into the first assembly of the term. The others had gone on ahead so it was just the two of them.

'Hello, Princess . . . I mean, Ameera,' Maria said as Sally brought her to sit with them. Did you sleep well?'

'I did, thank you. I have to say, though, there are an awful lot of animal noises outside during the night, aren't there?' Ameera said, yawning.

'That's the English countryside for you,' replied Molly.

'It might just be that they're animals you're not

used to hearing, so you notice it more. Can't imagine you get many owls hooting outside your window in India, do you?' Maria said.

'Do you know, I'm not sure. I don't think I've ever seen one. I think you might be right, though, about it all being strange to me. When I woke up this morning I had no idea where I was,' the princess said.

Maria thought how innocent she looked sitting there with the others in her blue check Garland summer dress. You might even say she looked *normal*. What was the faker hoping to achieve? That Ameera would make mistakes and embarrass herself? This was what she and the girls would have to find out before something awful happened. She couldn't explain why she sensed impending doom for the princess, but she did and it was a worry.

Suddenly, the room fell silent as an immaculate Madame Ruby swooshed onto the stage.

'Welcome, L'Etoilettes, to this new school term. As always, the summer term is a mix of exam nerves and academic and artistic triumphs. I know you will approach it with the intelligent calm and dedication I have come to expect from each of you.' She paused to smile at the sea of faces looking back at her.

'Now, first things first. I can't let this morning go

without making some introductions. A young lady who scarcely needs introducing . . . would you please, once again, give a warm welcome to Princess Ameera.' She paused as the room erupted into applause. 'As I explained briefly yesterday, the princess joins us for this term only, and wishes to have as many wonderful experiences as possible. Please do your utmost to include her in your activities, whether scholastic or social. Guide her and share with her as you would your own sister, so that she may go home fulfilled and with fond memories of her time here at L'Etoile. I must also ask that you all respectfully agree not to take any photographs of the princess at any time during her visit. This is a request directly from the prince's aides. Is that understood?'

All around her heads nodded solemnly.

Ameera was touched. *Your, L'Etoilette* had got Madame Ruby all wrong. She couldn't imagine her terrorising anyone!

'Now someone else I need to introduce you to is Miss Joshi, who joins L'Etoile temporarily to cover Miss Page's class, Three Alpha.'

Maria and the girls gasped.

'What is it?' Ameera whispered to Sally.

'Miss Page was our form tutor. She was awesome.

I can't believe she's not coming back this term. I wonder what's happened to her,' she whispered back.

'Quieten down, girls, please. I'm sorry to tell you that Miss Page had a skiing accident during the holidays and while she's on the mend, several broken bones will prevent her from returning to L'Etoile until later in the year.'

'Oh, poor Miss Page!' said Molly, thinking they must send her a *get well soon* card.

'What dreadful bad luck for us,' Honey said.

Madame Ruby went on. 'Miss Joshi joins us with a wealth of experience in teaching English as a foreign language and her international knowledge, having taught all over the world, is invaluable.'

Miss Joshi, who had stood up at the mention of her name, was a smiling, small Asian lady with her hair swept in soft curls to one side.

'First impressions?' Maria asked the others.

'Hmm . . . hard to tell. It's just so annoying Miss Page isn't here. She was ace!' Danya said. The girls had got on so well with their tutor. She was young and enthusiastic .

'I think Miss Joshi's a bit of a funny choice if you ask me. Why get someone whose background is teaching English as a foreign language? Not very L'Etoile is it?' Maria said.

'They might have wanted to make Ameera feel a little bit more comfortable. Makes sense for them to get someone on board who can link what she's been learning at home in India with what we've all been studying,' Pippa said.

The girls were impressed by her reasoning but didn't have time to dwell on the subject.

'And finally, a little bit of light relief for the term . . . the Summer Extravaganza, which will be held in the final week. I know it is customary for me to use this assembly to explain exactly what will be happening. However, this year, the staff and I have agreed that *you* should be the ones to choose what form it will take,' Madame Ruby continued as a little ripple of excitement went around the room. 'I'm prepared to consider any suggestions, provided it involves the whole school, so nothing too extreme, please. There will be an ideas box outside the staff room for the next forty-eight hours so get your thinking caps on and do your best to come up with something fabulous . . . ideally something we've never done before.'

The assembly hall was sizzling with chatter, everyone trying to think of something good enough for their idea to be chosen.

After letting them simmer for a moment, Madame

Ruby continued. 'It might even be nice to host an event or theme in honour of Princess Ameera, seeing as this Extravaganza will signify both the end of this school year and her stay with us at L'Etoile. Particularly if Prince Imran and Princess Preeti are able to join us.'

Another gasp went up.

Now that would be something to write home about, Story-seeker. Madame Ruby never failed to pull a rabbit out of a hat during the first assembly of term!

Ameera smiled at the hundreds of faces now staring at her, excited by the prospect of meeting her parents. *Mum and Dad coming here?* she thought. That was the first she'd heard about it. No doubt this was just something else her father had arranged and not had time to mention. Not that she was unhappy about being at L'Etoile – it had been her idea in the first place, but she was always being dispatched to one school or another. No matter how many times her mother reassured her it wasn't because she was adopted and therefore in need of more work than someone of royal blood would have been, Ameera couldn't help feeling it was. As if being a princess, being on show all the time wasn't enough pressure, having to work doubly hard to prove to everyone you could do it, just because you weren't born royal, made it so much harder.

'Shall we go, Ameera?' Sally said quietly.

As Sally showed the princess to their classroom, she thought how very normal she was. Even VIPs lose concentration sometimes and with that came the realisation that no one is perfect, no matter what their status, image or reputation.

'Good morning, everyone. Now if you'd all like to take your seats as quickly as you can, we'll begin. We've got a lot to get through this morning and as this is my first day I'll need as much guidance as you can offer!' Miss Joshi said calmly.

'Bullseye,' Maria whispered to Danya. *A teacher who needed guidance? Brilliant!*

'Hello, Miss Joshi. I'm Maria Fitzfoster,' Maria said confidently. 'Would you like us to stand up and introduce ourselves?'

'That would be most helpful. Thank you, Maria,' Miss Joshi said.

After the girls had finished, Miss Joshi turned to Ameera.

'Ameera, would you like to take a seat here near me at the front? That way we can muddle through as new girls together. While I'm not worried about any gaps in your studies, there will probably be quite a few new things to learn on the English curriculum that you won't have come across with your tutors at home,' Miss Joshi said, pointing to the only desk no one ever wanted to sit at for fear of *far too much teacher access*!

Ameera looked nervous at the thought of sitting up front alone.

'Will you come with me, Sally?' she whispered.

'Of course!' Sally said, kindly.

'Excellent,' Miss Joshi said. 'Now first of all, here are your exam timetables. You'll see they've been spread across a couple of weeks this year to give you plenty of revision time in between . . . ' she paused as Alice's hand shot up.

'Miss Joshi, I don't understand why there are history and English exams on this sheet. We've done coursework since the start of the year as Miss Page said she believes you get better results when you work steadily rather than under extreme pressure in a one-hour exam,' Alice said bravely.

'I see,' Miss Joshi said. 'I don't seem to have any notes on that here, Alice – I'll certainly make some enquiries. But in the meantime, try not to see exams as something to catch you out, rather to show what you know. The problem with doing coursework is that you have so much information at your fingertips to refer to, you never really get to demonstrate how much you've learned.'

'She's got a point,' Belle whispered to Alice. 'I practically copied my Easter history assignment straight from a similar essay I found online and if I'm honest, I don't remember any of it now.'

'What was that about an assignment?' Miss Joshi asked, hearing the tail end of Belle's conversation.

'Miss Page gave us a history essay to write, to count towards our results. They were to be handed in this morning,' Belle said, pulling hers out of her folder.

'Super. Marking those will give me the opportunity to get to know what you're all about. Can you pass them along?' Miss Joshi answered, eager to see what these girls were made of.

'I hope to goodness these count for our end-of-term result,' Pippa said, smoothing down her paper. 'I'm always so nervous about exams and I worked so hard on this history paper to max out my mark.'

'Well if the worst happens, I'll help you revise, Pips,' Maria said. 'You'll be fine.'

'Anyway, with a pop career like the one you're going to have, no one will give two hoots what mark you got in your third-year history exam!' Molly grinned.

Pippa felt boosted immediately.

'Thank you, everyone.' Miss Joshi collected up the last paper. 'Exam stress and how you learn to cope with it during your school years will prepare you for adult life, I promise.'

As Miss Joshi continued to talk to the class, Ameera focused on taking everything in. She didn't have a clue what this term, at this very British school, would entail but she was ready to find out. And Miss Joshi seemed nice. In fact she reminded her of one of her tutors at home. She'd spent most of her life being tutored privately or attending various foreign schools for short bursts, which didn't give her much time to make friends. The princess was a clever girl, but it was a lonely way to learn. She craved attending a school, with others her own age for companionship. That's why she was grateful for this term at L'Etoile. If she could leave with just one good friend to write to and perhaps invite for a visit, she'd be over the moon. And with Sally sitting beside her, she was well on the way to achieving it.

Ding, ding, the bell sounded for lunch.

'Goodness me, where did that time go?' Miss Joshi said, smoothing back her hair. 'What a whirlwind of questions and answers. I hope you found it as helpful as I did and I'll be sure to get to the bottom of this coursework/final exam query. Please don't forget to chat among yourselves about ideas for the Extravaganza. The clock is ticking on that and it would be marvellous if one of you Three Alpha girls could come up with the winning idea!'

The girls nodded and were out of the door before they'd even put their pens away.

'Well . . . what do you think, Mimi?' Molly asked her know-all sister.

'I think she's very nice,' Maria said. 'Considering what we could have ended up with!'

'Yes, she seems firm but fair, which is always good in a teacher. You know where you are with firm but fair. Mrs Fuller's like that too,' Pippa said.

'What do you think of Miss Joshi?' Sally asked Ameera as they walked to the Ivy Room.

'She's very helpful. I just hope I measure up!' Ameera said, a life-long concern for her in more ways than one.

6

Dear Diary . . .

*A*fter a busy couple of days settling in, Maria, Molly, Pippa and Sally were chilling in their room before lights out. Molly was plaiting her hair, Sally was reading, Pippa was scribbling lyrics in her notebook, wondering when she might get some feedback from Mr Fuller on what she'd sent in, and Maria was tapping away on her laptop.

'No more emails from the faker then?' Sally said, noticing Maria's frown.

'Not yet, but I'm not surprised. The faker would have expected me to get back online at the start of a new term. It would be too risky for them to email

Ameera straight away, in case I saw an answer to an email I never wrote!' Maria said.

'I just can't understand why anyone's doing it in the first place!' said Sally. 'What could they possibly have to gain?'

'I've been thinking about that,' Molly said. 'What if it's just a royal fan? Someone wanting to get close to the princess and be her friend? That might explain all the questions.'

'I love you, Molly, but don't forget that all those emails we read didn't sound as though they were from a fan. Someone seeking friendship wouldn't try to get her into trouble,' said Pippa.

'Then why?' Molly groaned.

'Hold on a sec, Ameera's just sent an email!' Maria said.

'Oh my goodness – in response to the faker?' Sally said, jumping up.

'No, actually I sent one myself last night trying to undo some of the damage that had been done by the faker. It wasn't easy, reversing things which had been said without Ameera realising I'm *Yours, L'Etoilette number two*!' Maria said.

'*Yours, L'Etoilette number one*, Mimi!' said Molly.

'Ha, of course!' Maria said.

'What's she saying then?' Pippa asked.

Maria scanned through the email. 'She's just answering some of my questions. I wanted to find out a bit more about her so we can help her enjoy her time here, so took a risk and fired some more questions at her. I figured she's more likely to tell *Yours, L'Etoilette* the truth than if we or a teacher ask her. I always get the feeling she says what she thinks everyone wants to hear.'

'Like what?' Molly asked.

'Listen . . .'

Dear Yours L'Etoilette, It's good to hear from you again. You sound cheerful. Are you happy to be back at school? It would be good to meet you in person . . .

'If only she knew!' Pippa smiled.

. . . but then again perhaps you're easier to talk to because it's not face to face. You think I'd be more guarded given that I don't know who it is I'm talking to but I've asked some of the other girls in my year about you and they have nothing but good things to say. Fashion

Faye in particular has said you're an absolute lifesaver, so I feel confident talking to you. It's like having a diary, only where the diary writes back overnight! You asked what inspires me . . . what drives me? Now that's a difficult question to answer honestly. While I get to see the most incredible things as a princess, I rarely get to DO anything myself. You know what I'd really like . . . really and truthfully? I'd like to play a game of football, dressed in a Chelsea kit – that's my secret favourite team. Not that I own a Chelsea kit . . . my family would have a fit! I'd like to have a water fight in the garden . . . a pillow fight in the bedroom . . . a midnight feast . . . in fact I'd like to do anything that feels like complete chaos. To cross the line. You might think it sounds silly but sometimes I'd love to go to the markets where I live and stroll about like everyone else. I'd like to select my own vegetables and spices, and take them back to the kitchens to cook. And that's where my real passion lies. Cooking is my absolute favourite thing to do. If I wasn't a princess, I'd have wanted to train as a Michelin-starred chef and travel the world cooking in the most prestigious restaurants, *wowing diners with my dishes, but sadly, there will never be a situation where my parents would allow me to cook for others. Never. Ever . . .*

'Hold on . . . rewind . . . did you say cook? She's a princess and she wants to cook?' Molly said, and ran over to the adjoining door.

Knock, knock, knockety, knock – this was the secret knock, so Honey and Danya knew it was them. In seconds the door swung open and in bounded the Sawyer twins in their PJs.

'Girls, you have to hear this. Read it again, Mimi, please,' Molly said. Honey and Danya listened, hardly believing their ears.

'I can't believe it. You'd have thought she had everything she wanted. She lives in a palace with all the clothes and jewels she could wish for. She could have a mani-pedi every day of her life if she wanted, and order the latest fashions before they even hit the shops!' Honey said, thinking about everything she'd do with her day if she was a princess.

'Yes, but I think that's her point. She can *have* and see anything she wants but she can't *do* everything that she wants to. As a princess, she's restricted about what she's allowed to do herself. Think about it. Princesses don't work up a sweat in the kitchen. They can request the best ingredients, the best chefs and eat the best foods, but they can't be seen to be cooking a meal themselves. And that's what Ameera wants: to do the things we take for granted,' Danya said.

'Gosh, if she fancies making my bed and tidying up my drawers every morning she should have just said so. Everyone's a winner,' Sally giggled.

The girls laughed but it was tinged with sadness. 'Read on, Mimi,' Molly urged.

Sometimes I wonder if I'm extra ambitious in ways I shouldn't be because, being adopted, I have normal blood. Perhaps that's why I dream of a normal life, to be free to do the things that everyone else does. I'm sure that's why Mum and Dad keep sending me to schools like L'Etoile, in the hope that I'll get things out of my system away from India, so as not to draw any unwanted attention at home. I know they think of me as their daughter and true heir, but I'm not so blind as to think that other members of the family wouldn't prefer someone of true royal blood to inherit my father's possessions. Oh but listen to me moaning on. I don't expect you to have any answers, Yours L'Etoilette, it's just nice to say it out loud. I wish

I was normal . . . there, I said it. I wish I was normal and not trapped by expectations of what is acceptable for a princess and what isn't. Anyway, thank you for listening.

Yours, Ameera.

'Wowsers,' Sally said, flumping back on her pillow.

'Who'd have thought all that was going on in that pretty little royal head of hers? She seems so . . . so sorted!' Pippa said.

'Never judge a book by its cover,' Honey said.

'So what do you do with a princess who doesn't want to be a princess?' Danya asked.

'Actually, I don't think it's that she doesn't want to be a princess – she just wishes there was a way of combining the two things,' Molly said, astutely.

'You're exactly right, Molly, and we're going to make it our mission for Ameera to experience the things she longs for during her time with us,' said Maria, before hitting print and then delete on Ameera's email, just in case the faker were to log in and see it!

Wouldn't want that falling into the wrong hands, would we, Story-seeker?

'We're going to have to be really clever about how we create all these opportunities, though,' Danya said. 'If, as she says, she never voices these desires out loud, and we start bringing them up in conversation, she'll know we're *Yours, L'Etoilette* in seconds.'

'That's why we're going to pretend they're our secret desires, not hers,' Maria said.

'What does that mean?' Molly asked.

'Hey wait, I can hear them now . . . .' Pippa said. 'The cogs turning to make one of Maria's brainwaves.'

'And when exactly are you going to tell us what's going on this time? Before it happens or while it's happening, as usual?' Molly said.

'Just so long as it ends up with us scooting around in the dark sporting our black assassin gear, I'm in!' Honey said excitedly.

'You'll see,' Maria said. 'You'll see.'

7

A Plan Comes Together

The forty-eight hour deadline for students to come up with plans for the end-of-term entertainment was looming. Only a couple of hours to go and the girls had been so busy that Maria hadn't had a single moment to discuss her idea with the others. There was nothing else for it: she was going to have to go for it and just hope they thought it was good!

Miss Joshi had finished telling the girls that their coursework would form the majority of their final marks for the year, which they were in raptures about, so Maria thought she'd take her chance.

'Miss Joshi? Before we go, I wonder if we might have a quick class chat about an idea the girls and I have had for the Extravaganza,' she said, ignoring the looks of *Our idea . . . oh really?* from Molly and the others.

'Wonderful, Maria. Do go on,' Miss Joshi said, perching on the corner of her desk.

'Well, Molly and I were talking last night about when we went to watch *The Great British Bake Off* being filmed . . .

'Anyway, to cut a long story short, instead of putting on the usual talent contest, why don't we have a bake-off competition and combine it with some sort of performance,' Maria said, but she was starting to get funny looks from the rest of the class.

'No offence, Maria, but this is a school for the performing arts – do any of us know about cooking? I know I don't,' Lara said.

'Me neither,' Amanda said.

Danya, who'd been listening, cottoned on quickly and could see a gap in Maria's pitch to the class. She jumped to the rescue.

'What Maria's saying is this: what if, as Madame Ruby suggested, we theme this in honour of Ameera. As we are so lucky to have the princess in our year, it makes sense for us to come up with an Indian-themed Extravaganza.' Danya paused to check the rest of the class were with her, which they were. 'And what's at the heart of Indian culture if not its national cuisine! What if we were to come up with a delicious Indian meal followed by some sort of homage through song and dance?'

'Exactly, Dan!' Maria exclaimed. She could have kissed her friend.

'It'll look fabulous. I can see it now, a Bollywood-esque Extravaganza!' Molly said, buzzing with how it would look on the stage, a multitude of brilliant colours.

'Right!' Maria and Danya said at once.

'What if we just left out the cooking thing? I don't really get that part,' Lara said again. 'We could still have an Indian Extravaganza – just keep it musical. None of us can cook, and I think we'll just be setting ourselves up for a fall.'

'Actually, I can cook,' came a quiet voice from the front of the room.

'Ameera?' Miss Joshi said in surprise. 'I'm sorry, I thought you just said you cook.'

'Yes. I do, actually. I just don't get the chance very often,' Ameera continued. 'I'd love to help with that part and I've had Bollywood dance training so could help with that too. Just don't ask me to sing. I'd fall off the stage with fright!'

'Bingo!' Danya whispered to Honey.

'Perfect!' Maria shouted before anyone could put her off. 'That's settled then. I'll write it up now and pop it in the box before it closes.'

'Just one thing, girls,' Miss Joshi asked. 'How would the rest of the school be involved in this?'

The girls sat in silence for a moment, then Ameera put up her hand.

'They could do different countries,' she said. 'Each year can come up with a menu and musical performance which represents their chosen country.'

'That's brilliant!' Sally said. 'How can Madame Ruby refuse? It's genius. What better way to celebrate our international community here at the school than by taking the audience on a culinary and cultural journey around the world!'

'Yes, and the winning year group would be announced at the end of the show. Obviously the audience can't all try the food. That part of the competition would happen the morning of the event and they'd just have to trust the judges,' Maria said.

'Let's agree for that judge not to be Mrs Mackle, though! We need someone with a finer palate!' Belle said and everyone giggled.

'All right girls,' Miss Joshi said. 'Is everyone

happy?' The girls nodded, their eyes twinkling with excitement. 'And as it seems to me that you will be in charge of the menu, are you absolutely sure about this, Ameera?' Miss Joshi said.

Say yes! Say yes! Maria thought under her breath, exasperated by Miss Joshi trying to remind the princess that cookery might not be the sort of thing her family sent her to L'Etoile to perfect.

Ameera took a massive breath. 'One thousand per cent yes!' she cried.

It was now or never. When would an opportunity like this ever cross her path again? She could hardly believe it. A chance to work wonders in a kitchen without having to sneak about to do it. At home she only ever cooked if her parents were away and she convinced the kitchen staff to keep it quiet – which they did because they always enjoyed devouring her food at the end of it. The only thing bothering her was if her parents did indeed visit for the Extravaganza. That would be interesting. Still, she had options. She could pretend, as usual, she'd just had the ideas behind it, rather than the chef. In an ideal world, she'd finally get to be honest with them. Maybe then they'd see what a princess was really capable of and applaud her for it.

'There's no more to be said on the subject then. Well done, girls. Especially you, Maria,' Miss Joshi said.

As predicted, Madame Ruby and Mrs Fuller thought Three Alpha's idea was superb. Cookery had never been considered a performing art, but even Mrs Fuller had to admit Maria put forward a very strong case.

'It takes immense talent and creativity to put together a dish that will wow a panel of judges and we think we have the perfect people in Three Alpha to be able to pull this off. Princess Ameera is already involved and with Faye doing the costumes, the dancers working out our choreography and Pippa penning a new Bollywoodesque song, we can't fail to take the crown . . . excuse the pun!'

'And you're sure Ameera is happy to lead the cookery side of things?' Madame Ruby said. *A chef princess? Whoever heard of such a thing?* she thought.

'It was her idea!' Maria said quickly.

*Well, strictly speaking,
that was true, Story-seeker!*

'I think it's marvellous, Maria. Well done,' Madame Ruby smiled.

'I'll send a note to the other tutors right away so the year groups can let me have their chosen countries. There won't be much time for everyone to rehearse, what with exam revision, so they'll have to get cracking,' said Mrs Fuller.

'Brilliant!' Maria said. 'May I go?'

'Of course. I'll let Mrs Mackle know to expect a list of ingredients to order shortly. It wouldn't do for the princess to arrive in an unstocked kitchen, now would it?' Mrs Fuller said with a smile.

'Absolutely not!' Maria said, turning to go.

'Oh, but one very important thing to tell your chef, Maria. The school has a no-nuts policy. Nut allergies are so common these days, it's better to be safe than sorry. In actual fact, I suffer quite badly myself. You'll have noticed there was no marzipan in my wedding cake!' Mrs Fuller said.

If you remember, Story-seeker, our girls actually attended Mrs Fuller's wedding to music industry guru Emmett Fuller, as Pippa had been invited to sing for them in the church.

'Yes, but you had a chocolate wedding cake, which beats boring old fruit and nut cake any day of the week!' Maria answered. 'No nuts! Got it! Thanks so much, Mrs Fuller.'

And she raced back to Garland to give the girls the good news.

'So what's next, you master schemer you?' Molly teased her sister.

'What do you mean?' Maria said.

'How many other dreams are you going to make come true for our princess?'

'One miracle at a time, Molly dear.'

'Hi, Molly!' said Honey as she popped her head through the adjoining door. 'Did you tell the girls about our album idea?'

'Not yet, no. I've already started working on it, though. I got a brilliant shot of Ameera in the library surrounded by about twenty cookery books this afternoon. Look, it's fab – you can barely see her face peeping over the top, they're stacked so high,' Molly said, scrolling through her digital camera.

'What's this for?' Pippa said. 'I thought photos of

the princess were banned!'

'You tell them, Honey,' Molly said.

'OK. Molly and I thought it would be nice to take secret photos of Ameera doing all the things she'll want to remember when she goes home. Then when we go to say goodbye at the end of term, we can give her an album, and all the memory cards and stuff so she doesn't worry — and nor does Madame Ruby — about what we're going to do with them. It'll help her remember her L'Etoile days,' Honey said.

'That's so thoughtful, guys,' said Danya. 'She'll love it. I wish we'd done something similar to document our time here. It would be cool to look back at the early days now.'

'Ah it would, you're right. But we have each other to gossip with and keep those memories alive. Once Ameera goes home, she'll be on her own again. That's why, if we get this right, it might just be the best present she's ever had,' said Honey.

'Very cool, girls. And in answer to your last question, let's see now, what was on her list?' said Maria, pulling out a printout of Ameera's email. 'Ah yes, a couple of fights to instigate — water and pillow! That shouldn't take too much organising. Just a well-managed midnight feast and a hot sunny weekend!'

'We're going to be busy!' Sally said.

'And in trouble!' Pippa said, wondering how they were going to get away with it all.

'Not if we're careful. What if we get Miss Joshi in on a couple of them? If we explain what we're trying to do for Ameera and that it's all in the name of fun, she just might *chaperone* us – well, some of it anyway,' Maria said.

'If you think she'd be up for it, then I'm in!' Danya said.

'I'm not sure you're thinking clearly about this, guys. Get a teacher involved? Are you crazy?' Pippa said.

'Don't worry, Pips. It'll all work out – I promise! I now declare Operation Dream-maker in motion!' Molly said.

'Woooohooo!'

8

Operation Dream-Maker

s it turned out, Miss Joshi wasn't their biggest problem. Butch was. Everywhere Ameera was, there was Butch standing ten paces behind, watching over her like a ferocious guard dog just in case anything should happen.

'I don't think Miss Joshi's the one we need to win over, Maria,' Molly said as they swerved around Butch waiting for Ameera outside the music rooms.

'I know, he's everywhere,' Maria said. 'There's no getting anything past him. He's too good at his job!'

'How are we going to sneak her into our room for tonight's midnight feast? I've got it all ready and Sally's gone to the office to collect a hamper of goodies her Mum cooked up especially for the occasion.'

'I agree – it's not Miss Joshi we need to get onside. I think we need to talk to Butch. We're never going to get round him otherwise. He sticks to her like glue!' Danya said.

'Do you think he'll be up for it?' Maria said.

'Let's hope so, for Ameera's sake, or she's never going to have any fun. So long as he knows where she is at all times he can fulfil his duty and keep her safe. We'll tell him he can have men outside the bedroom windows if he likes, in case he thinks we're going to escape down knotted bed-sheets or something,' said Danya.

'OK. I'll do it after music. Wish me luck!' Maria said, trotting into the Mozart Rooms to practise her exam piece.

It was just as well Maria was such a natural at most things, Story-seeker, as this princess mission was taking up rather a lot of her time. At least the Yours L'Etoilette faker seemed to have disappeared from the scene . . . for the moment.

'Well, what did he say?' Danya asked as Maria came into the Ivy Room for lunch after a lengthy conversation with Butch.

'He was a bit shocked, but I'm sure I saw a little smile creep across his face at one point. I just asked him to give us a chance to earn his trust and that we only wanted to give Ameera a few fun memories,' said Maria, feeling pleased with herself.

'Well done, Mimi!' Molly said, hugging her sister.

'So we're on then? A double treat – midnight feast plus a pillow fight,' Pippa said. She'd never had a pillow fight herself so this would be a first for her too.

'Mum sent me down a real feather pillow for Ameera for the occasion and I've loosened some of the stitches, so at some point that little baby's going to explode all over the place. Thought it would make a really good photo!' Honey whispered to Molly.

Sally, having overheard Honey's brainwave, wondered who was going to clear *that little baby* up once the game was over!

By ten p.m., thinking they'd get as much *midnight* feast time in as possible, Ameera was munching away on Maggie Sudbury's legendary chocolate brownies, pleading with Sally to get her the recipe.

'I can't believe you've never had a midnight feast, Ameera,' Honey said.

'Well I, for one, am honoured to be throwing your first!' Sally said, taking a big gulp of her favourite freshly squeezed pink lemonade.

'Molly, have you got a date for your premiere yet?' Pippa asked.

'Yes actually!' Molly said.

'A premiere? For what?' Ameera asked.

'My ever-so-talented actress sister here managed to land herself a starring role in the new Warner Brothers film!' Maria said.

'Really?' Ameera said. 'Wow, how cool!'

Molly was touched the princess should be impressed about something she'd done.

'It's not that big a deal really, but it was fun. I can't wait to see it. When you're filming, they don't always shoot everything in order, so it's hard to get a feel for what the film will be like,' said Molly, trying her hardest to be humble.

'Where's it going to be?' said Ameera, wishing immediately she could go too.

'It's in London on the nineteenth of December. In

Leicester Square!' Molly said.

'I've heard about Leicester Square. Isn't that where all the big Hollywood movie premieres happen?' asked Ameera.

'Yes! I can't wait. You should come over for it!' Molly said, thinking how amazing it would be to introduce a princess to everyone.

'Oh my gosh, that would be a dream come true, but I doubt I'd be allowed,' Ameera said. 'Not sure my parents would deem that an appropriate outing for a princess.'

'Well, don't give up yet. We've been known to perform the odd miracle in the past,' Pippa said. 'You never know what the future might bring when you're at L'Etoile! What is it old Ruby always says?'

Reach for the stars, L'Etoilettes, reach for the stars!' the girls all cried at once in their best Madame Ruby voices.

'What are you going to wear?' Honey said suddenly, her face deadly serious.

'Are you really going to ask that question, Honey? Now? Half a year before it's even happening?' said Danya, rolling her eyes, before launching a well-aimed cushion at her sister's head. It was the perfect opportunity to start the pillow fight.

Honey gasped and leapt off the bed to grab Ameera's special pillow and one for herself. By the time she returned, it was war. Brownies and popcorn everywhere followed by a cloud of feathers once Ameera dared to throw her pillow into the fray. What a picture! (And Molly made sure she took plenty!)

'OK! OK! I surrender,' Pippa said at last.

'Me too!'

'Me three!'

'Oh my goodness,' Ameera said. I don't think I've ever had this much fun – or made this much mess! How are we going to clear this up before the morning?' she gasped, picking half a dozen feathers out of her long dark hair.

'Ah ha!' Maria said in delight as she whipped out the latest super-turbo hand-held vacuum from under her bed. 'Fear not, L'Etoilettes! I'll have this place spotless in seconds!'

'A vacuum? Are you for real?' Molly smiled.

'We can all make an online purchase, Molly dear, it's just I prefer to gadget shop while you're clothes shopping.'

'I think we'd better leave the tidy-up until the morning, unless you're going to tell me that vacuum has a silencer on it?' Danya said, raising an eyebrow.

*Maria had a knack for achieving
the impossible, Story-seeker.*

'Actually, Miss Sawyer . . .' Maria began.

Danya's jaw hit the ground.

'Just kidding! Sounds like a lawnmower! Definitely a job for tomorrow,' Maria grinned.

'I'd better get back to my room. Can't believe you got . . . what do you call him?' Ameera asked.

'Butch!' Sally giggled.

'Ha! Yes, Butch. Can't believe you got him to agree to let me sneak out like this. I'll have to try that myself next time,' Ameera said.

'There's about ten men on the ground outside though,' Pippa said, sneaking a peek out of the window.

'I'll bet there are!' Ameera said. 'I'd best get back to my room and get everything ready for our fashion show tomorrow!'

'Yes! Don't forget about that. We're so excited about coming to try on all your stuff!' Molly said gleefully, having practically bitten Ameera's hand off when she offered some of her wardrobe for the girls to wear in the Extravaganza. Faye was particularly pleased as it meant she didn't have so much prep to do for the show.

'I won't. Good night, girls, and thank you so much for a brilliant night,' Ameera said before disappearing silently down the corridor, a smiling Butch in tow.

'Success?' Molly asked, beaming at the state of the room.

'A triumph!' Danya said.

'Night girls. Love you all!' Honey whispered as she and Danya sneaked back through the adjoining door and clicked the lock.

'Think we're going to need more than a turbo vacuum to sort this lot out,' Sally said in despair.

'Worth it, though . . . to see the look on her face when her pillow exploded, right?'

'Definitely!'

9

The Great Indian Makeover

℘rincess Ameera had gone through the whole day with a spring in her step. She was absolutely thrilled by last night's hilarious pillow fight and wondered what she could do for the girls in return. Her first thought was to get them all tickets to see a musical in London or something. Perhaps Mrs Kapoor would get permission from her parents to chaperone them if they could get a weekend in London before the end of term, but to be honest, the days were whizzing by so fast and she wasn't sure there would be time. What she would dearly like to have done was to get tickets to the next Chelsea football game, but she couldn't really see Honey or Molly being particularly pleased about that, nor could she bring herself to admit her love of football and all things Chelsea to anyone. No, she'd just have to try to question the girls about what they liked to do, without giving anything away, and then make it happen.

The other thing she had to concentrate on was coming up with a suitable menu for the cookery competition. Given the school nut ban, she was struggling to think what to cook. She couldn't believe she was going to do it! She had one shot at impressing everyone, including possibly her parents, so the menu was everything. The only thing that might prevent her mum and dad going ballistic at her for having actually done the cooking herself, would be if the food was too delicious for them not to be uncontrollably proud of her.

Part of her didn't believe they would make it to L'Etoile for the end of term Extravaganza anyway. In fact, during the last conversation she'd had with her mother at the start of the week, she'd promised Ameera that they were doing everything in their power to make it happen – which usually meant that when the day came, *something unforeseen*, or something which was *just one of those things* would always happen to stop them being there. She knew it wasn't intentional; it just went with the territory of being the daughter of two supremely important and busy people. Usually it didn't really bother her, but then *usually* she didn't allow herself to become so involved at other schools she'd visited. She couldn't put her finger on why she felt so much a part of L'Etoile. Perhaps because she'd never been so welcomed before, and that was all thanks to Sally and the girls. Suddenly, the *aloof Indian princess*, as she'd often overheard people call her, was not only devising and executing a menu, but choreographing and directing a Bollywood dance sequence and, any minute now, would be opening her wardrobe doors to her entire school year for a mammoth Indian makeover! She hardly knew herself.

Knock, knock . . .

'Come in!' Ameera called as Butch opened the door to Molly and Honey, who were ready to burst with excitement. They couldn't believe they were being given the opportunity to raid a princess's wardrobe!

'Oh, Princess,' Molly exclaimed. 'Is it time?'

Ameera giggled. 'Yes, Miss Fitzfoster and Miss Sawyer, it's time!' She'd never known anyone as obsessed with clothes and beauty as these two. 'Are you quite sure you're not sisters? You're more like each other than like Maria and Danya!'

'Ah, really? Thanks,' Honey said, taking that as a compliment.

'Hello, Ameera,' a voice said from the corridor.

'Sorry Faye!' Molly said, having forgotten they'd brought Faye along.

'Hi Faye, I've heard all about your beautiful costumes and seen some of the photos of past years' events in the assembly hall. You're so clever! I hope you're not too put out that I said the girls could borrow some of my outfits this year,' Ameera said as Faye blushed.

'Absolutely not! In fact I couldn't be more grateful that I'm going to have an unusually stress-free end of year, which never happens, believe me! Usually I'm having a dress-making meltdown by now. You've literally saved me from a week of sleepless nights,' Faye said.

'It's my pleasure. There's definitely more than enough to go around . . . twice if necessary!' Ameera said, nodding at the clothes hanging around the room and spilling out of the wardrobes.

'I just can't believe it!' Molly said, like a child in a

sweetshop. 'It's such an honour. I'll remember this day for ever.'

'Oh Molly, you're too adorable. Help yourself!' Ameera said. Their enthusiasm was infectious. 'And if you think this is good, you should come over to India. I've got a walk-in wardrobe the size of the Ivy Room!'

Molly looked as if she might pass out at the thought. 'Come on, Moll,' Honey said.

'Ameera, I've done a schedule for the rest of the year to come in in pairs to try on their outfits. Once I've had a good look through everything, it shouldn't take too long. I pretty much know everyone's size and shape by heart so will know what suits before they even get here. Just one question, though: would it be all right if I took a polaroid photo of each girl when she's dressed, so that I can put together a "look book" for the event? That's what I usually do. It's the best way to keep track of who's wearing what on the day,' Faye said.

Ameera turned pale at the mention of photographs being taken in her bedroom. 'Sure, but please don't take any shots with me in the background or anything. I'm not sure what my parents would think about me hosting a *fancy dress* party with all my royal clothes. I'd be in a world of trouble if any pictures got out!'

'Of course,' Faye said. 'I never even thought about that.'

'Thanks. I just have to be so careful. The press has only ever printed pictures that have been carefully selected by my parents . . . official shots of me in a tiara looking bored to tears . . . you know the type of thing.' Ameera paused as Faye nodded. 'I think they have to be extra cautious about my actions and behaviour in the public eye because I'm adopted. It's not my parents personally who are worried or ashamed – they know I won't do anything to let them down, but there are some family members who'd prefer that a prince or princess of true royal blood eventually takes my father's place.'

'Wow, that is serious stuff!' Molly said, having caught on to the conversation, mid try-on.

'But who would be spiteful enough to do that? Especially someone in your own family,' Honey asked.

Ameera's cheeks burned. She'd said too much, she knew she had, but there was something about these girls that made her want to pour out her heart to them.

'It's just my uncle. My father's brother. I don't think he's ever got over the fact that he and then his son won't ever inherit my father's wealth since my parents adopted me,' said Ameera.

'Well, he's just going to have to get used to the idea, isn't he?' Molly said, placing the most beautiful jewel-encrusted tiara on Ameera's head.

'I don't even want to know if that thing's real!' Honey exclaimed, eyeing up the size of the jewels twinkling on it.

'I do!' Molly said. 'Ameera, can I just get one photo of me wearing that? I might never get the chance again!'

'Sure!' Ameera said and placed it in the centre of Molly's golden locks. 'Arise, Princess Molly!' she commanded and Faye clicked her camera.

Knock, knock . . .

'That'll be Lottie and Sofia and I haven't even had a chance to go through everything yet!' Faye said.

'Look, don't worry, Faye. We'll do it between us. You take Lottie round and I'll take Sofia,' Ameera said, delighted to have the chance to get to know some of the other girls a bit better too. 'How long did you say we have between visitors?'

'Twenty-minute slots,' Faye said, bristling with pride at having the chance to work so closely with Princess Ameera.

'Perfect,' she said, making for the door. 'Lottie, Sofia! Welcome. Are you ready for your Bollywood makeover? Then let's go!' Ameera said, loving every second.

The room erupted in a swirl of colour as the entire third year came and went, each girl revelling in the experience a little more than the last. Beautiful silk tunics and scarfs, all colours of the rainbow, smothered in patterns of swirling gold thread. After Honey and Maria had exhausted every inch of the royal wardrobe, they took it in turns to wait outside in the corridor to catch every girl on their way out and ask them to record a video message for Ameera. Butch watched in amusement as they all raved about meeting the princess and wished her well for the future. He had no idea what Molly and Honey planned to do with all those messages, but couldn't see the harm in keeping it from the princess. So long as she didn't appear in any footage, he was doing his job.

Pippa, Sally, Danya and Maria were the last four students to arrive, secretly slightly concerned that all the best outfits might have been taken. But they needn't have worried, for there, hanging on the picture rail, were the most beautiful Indian saris they'd ever seen.

'What do you think, gang? Honey and I picked these out for you before any of the others arrived.'

'Yes – Dan – this golden yellow will be perfect on you,' Honey said, grabbing it for her sister to try on.

'I love it!' Danya said.

'Oh my, is that real gold thread?' Pippa asked as Ameera handed her an emerald-green outfit to match her eyes.

'Erm, yes, I think it might be,' Ameera said shyly.

'Wow, thanks for lending us all these,' Maria said. 'You really didn't have to . . . but, and no offence Faye, I think even you couldn't have come up with anything this beautiful in the time we have.'

'I'm not even going to bother denying it!' Faye said. 'Everyone's going to look amazing – and that blue silk will look stunning on you, Maria!'

Sally was nervously shifting from side to side. *Oh no, they forgot my outfit! Now I'll have to pick from whatever no one else wanted.*

'Sally!' Ameera said suddenly. 'Don't look so glum. I chose yours before any of the girls arrived – even Molly and Honey haven't seen this one!'

Molly and Honey both twitched.

Sally felt her eyes prick with tears. 'You did?' she

said, her gaze following Ameera as she opened the wardrobe doors.

'Tah-dah!' Ameera said, and hanging in her hand was the most beautiful outfit of all. It was white with silver thread and hundreds of tiny pearls.

Sally couldn't believe her eyes. 'You picked that out for me? Oh my goodness. Are you sure? I mean, shouldn't you be wearing that?'

'No. This one's got your name on it. Now come try it on,' Ameera instructed and then whispered to Sally, 'It's always customary to save the best until last!'

'Oh thank you so much, Princess,' Sally said. 'You've made me feel like . . . like a princess!'

'And you've made me feel like a friend, and I can't thank you enough for all your kindness,' Ameera said, giving Sally a hug.

'Wow, you all look amazing!' Faye said. 'Stand together and let's get a Polaroid for the look book. Everyone say "bhajis"!'

'Bhajis!' they called out and fell about laughing.

What an evening to remember!

10

Fun in the Kitchen

Now that the third years looked the part, it was time to focus on the actual entertainment for their Indian-themed Extravaganza entry. While the rest of the year were working on their Bollywood dancing, Pippa had written some lyrics for the occasion, and Maria accompanied her on the piano. Between them they'd come up with a pretty great track, even if they did say so themselves.

'We should collaborate more often!' Pippa said as Maria played her out.

'Agreed. It's been fun. Sometimes I'm so busy scheming, I forget that I'm supposed to be at L'Etoile to study music!' said Maria.

'You are funny. I never stop thinking about music. If I'm awake, I'm humming to myself—' Pippa started.

'And if you're asleep, you're humming to yourself!' said Maria.

'No way! You never said. Do I really sing in my sleep?'

'Sometimes. But we love it, which is why we've never told you. It's not every night. Just when you're under pressure with your writing. The worst it ever got was after Mrs Fuller asked you to write a song for her wedding. You used to sing whole songs in your sleep in the weeks leading up to that moment!'

'I can't believe it. I'm a crazy person!' said Pippa.

'Well if you are, then that makes me crazy too,' Ameera said, suddenly appearing in the doorway. 'I cook and eat whole meals in my sleep. Sometimes it's so vivid I even wake up feeling stuffed!'

'I'm in good company then!' said Pippa. 'Hi, Ameera. How's the choreography going? Are the girls picking it up quickly?'

'It's quite a new style for them, but yes, they're doing really well,' Ameera said.

'Ameera, tell me. Do you sing?' Pippa asked, suddenly having a brainwave.

Ameera looked panicked. 'Cooking, yes; dancing,

yes; singing, not in a million years. I told you that already. I'd fall off the stage with fright.'

'Why do you ask, Pips? What are you thinking?' said Maria.

'Just that it would be great to have an Indian vocal running through the background of this track. I've watched so many Bollywood music videos, but just can't get the right sound and a second, authentic voice would be out of this world.'

'She's right, Ameera. Not that we want to push you to do anything, but why don't you listen to the track and see if anything comes naturally. Never know!' Maria said, wondering if they might have hit upon another secret princess craving.

'Here, take this. I've just burned a CD. It's got our Bollywood track first and then there are a few others I've been working on this year. The second one, 'Hands Up', is one my uncle and I wrote and produced in the summer and it's going to be One Direction's new release!' Pippa said proudly.

'What?' Maria and Ameera said in unison.

'AYKM?' Maria exclaimed.

'Maria Fitzfoster! Did you just do a Molly?' Pippa said, aghast.

'Well, if there was ever a time, this is it! She'll faint

when she hears about this!' Maria grinned.

'Sorry – Ameera,' Pippa said, noticing Ameera's confusion. 'AYKM? is Molly for *are you kidding me*?'

'I see. I absolutely agree! One Direction! Wow! That's quite an achievement, Miss Burrows!' said Ameera.

'Why thank you, Your Royal Highness! I didn't say, because Mr Fuller swore me to secrecy until they'd sent out the press release, but if it helps persuade a certain Indian princess to duet with me, it's worth it,' Pippa said with a smile.

'What can I say?' Ameera said. 'Who am I to deny my little voice to the great One Direction's song writer? Hand it over. I'll listen tonight and if my vocal chords aren't too rusty, I'll give it a go. Might have to work out a way I can hide on stage if we do it, though.'

'We'll think of something!' Maria said. 'We'll get together in music tomorrow and you can let us know what you've decided. We've got to nail this and submit our score to Mr Potts by nine o'clock tomorrow morning. He's been chasing me all week. Apparently we're the only ones not to have given him our music for the orchestra to learn.'

'Sure, no problem. And thanks for this, Pippa. I can't wait to hear it all,' Ameera said.

'Hope you like it!'

'I'd like to know if I like it,' Maria said, pretending to be annoyed. 'But I can't do that if I'm not allowed to hear it. Wait until I tell the others you've let your new royal friend listen to a future 1D track before they have. Wouldn't like to be in your shoes, Pippa Burrows.'

'Maria, you wouldn't!' Pippa said in a panic.

'Oh wouldn't I?' Maria said before running off with Pippa hot on her heels.

As the weeks passed, the school was bustling with last-minute exam revision and group rehearsals. All in all it had been a good term, particularly for our girls. Apart from the ever-present threat that the faker might re-surface, they were basking in the glow of royalty. Maria was still checking the *Yours, L'Etoilette* account every hour, almost willing the faker to send another email to the princess revealing some evil grand plan. It was almost a disappointment that the mystery seemed to have fizzled out.

'I hate that we never got to the bottom of who the faker was, or is. It niggles me all the time!' Maria said to Danya while they were in the quad, classifying and watering plants for their biology homework.

'I know! It totally goes against everything we stand for. No stone unturned and all that. Do you think we'll hear something again soon?' Danya filled a small watering can.

'Not sure. Even Ameera has stopped emailing *Yours, L'Etoilette* now, which might explain why the faker's not bothering to hack in anymore,' said Maria.

'Well that's a good thing, isn't it? Perhaps she feels she's finally replaced an imaginary e-friendship with real ones. Namely, *us*!' Danya said.

'Hey!' came a shriek from Alice. 'Belle Brown, you're supposed to be watering the herb garden, not me!'

Maria's eyes flashed with mischief. It was time for another of the princess's secret wishes.

'Dan!' Maria whispered suddenly, 'I'm going to explode with boredom if things don't start hotting up around here! You with me?'

'How do you mean?' Danya said, wondering what this next move entailed.

'You'll catch on,' Maria said with a grin. 'Just follow my lead!'

And with that, Maria grabbed one of the potting trays, filled it with pond water, and calmly emptied it all down Molly's back! Molly swung round in shock, about to hit the roof, but luckily caught Maria's eye.

Well, she started it! Water fight!

'It's not funny, Mimi!' Molly said, quickly improvising to give her an excuse to react. 'How would you like it?' she said, launching her bucket of muddy water right back at her sister, before bursting into a fit of giggles as a clod of soggy soil splatted onto Maria's left shoulder.

'Hey! That got me!' yelled Pippa, grabbing the hose and spraying it high into the air to get as many girls as she could in one hit. Seconds later she was drenched from behind by Sally's well-aimed bucket.

'Really, Sally? You really want to take me on while I'm holding the hose?' Pippa said, smoothing down her soaking wet hair.

And with that she changed the setting on the hose nozzle to *shower* and soaked Sally from head to toe.

Ameera, who was standing next to Sally in utter amazement, suddenly burst out laughing and threw the contents of her own watering can at Pippa.

That was it. On seeing the princess's involvement, every third year started firing water-shots at each other for no good reason, other than the fact that they wanted to join in the fun. And within about thirty seconds the quad was the scene of the wettest and funniest water fight in the history of L'Etoile.

The usually immaculate, now saturated lawns were quickly becoming a mud bath and were more slippery than an ice rink, demonstrated beautifully by Mr Hart, who had appeared to stop the chaos, only to skid right into the middle of the crossfire.

Twinkle, on the other hand, was having the time of her life, racing through the spray and leaving muddy paw prints everywhere.

Honey and Molly once again took it in turns to secretly capture photos of the princess having the time of her life at the messiest event she'd ever attended. She looked so happy they could have cried.

Suddenly the fire alarm sounded, stopping everyone in their tracks, and Mrs Fuller stood at the top of the path. The girls didn't think they'd ever seen her look so angry – they could almost see steam coming out of her ears.

'I am utterly speechless!' Mrs Fuller said. 'You will go to your rooms immediately to dry off and get changed. Then you will all return here and attempt to repair some of the damage you have done. And I don't want to hear one word spoken. Do I make myself clear?'

There was silence. Even the sight of poor, dripping wet Mr Hart and a bedraggled Twinkle didn't raise a giggle. They were all in trouble, but at least it would be impossible for anyone to be singled out, so the whole year would bear the responsibility and punishment for what had been *the best* biology class ever!

'Can you believe that just happened? Maria, I could have belted you when you threw that water down my back,' Molly said as she towel-dried her hair.

'Even I didn't expect such a result!' Maria said. 'Ameera's face was an absolute picture!'

'It couldn't have gone any better. I notice Butch didn't wade in and stop it,' Danya said.

'Can you blame him – that Armani suit would never have been the same again!' Molly said.

'Miss Joshi just stood there too. I think she was in shock. She didn't even try to get involved!' Sally said.

'It was a bit wild, girls,' Pippa said. 'I wasn't sure there was going to be an end to it at one point.'

'You can always rely on Mrs Fuller to drag us back to reality. That fire alarm trick worked a treat. I'll have to think of a way of disabling that next time,' said Maria.

'Next time?' Pippa said in a panic.

As the summer term went on, it was business as usual at L'Etoile – preparing for exams which seemed never-ending, but thankfully mixed with some chill-out time. Our girls spent theirs writing and receiving emails from home, which brought the most gorgeous photos of baby Flori and some mouth-watering goodies to share from Sally's mum, Maggie. Another favourite pastime – particularly for Molly and Honey, was online shopping and sneaking out to get deliveries from the delightful Albie Good, who was the delivery boy for *www.looklikeastar.com*. Albie spent more time delivering to Molly and the girls at L'Etoile than he did to any other customer. He was more like a member of the family – particularly since he'd helped them so much during their investigations and exposure of a smuggling ring operating at the Fitzfoster family home in Sussex the summer before. Every time he made a delivery, Molly and Honey ran straight to Ameera with their new clothes and accessories, eager for her approval on everything.

In no time at all there were only days to go until the end of term Extravaganza, and the whole school was in show mode, whether it was rehearsals on stage or in the school kitchens, perfecting their menus for Thursday morning's judging.

Most of the students who'd elected to cook had been forced to use the boarding-house kitchens and staffroom kitchen to practise their menus, as Mrs Mackle, the school cook, couldn't bear to have students running around her kitchen. But Princess Ameera (and her sous-chef, Sally Sudbury) were, of course, a different story and had been given full run of the Ivy Room kitchen. Mrs Mackle watched in delight as Ameera chopped and sliced and fried and diced the most exquisite array of Indian cuisine and, of course, got to sample everything she cooked.

'Who taught you to cook, Ameera?' Mrs Mackle asked as she watched her marinate some chicken thighs in exotic spices and oils.

'I don't know, really. I'm obsessed with cookery programmes and when I'm not studying I like to hang out in the kitchen and watch the chefs prepare for our banquets.'

'What made you decide on these ingredients, these particular dishes, when you've so much to choose from?' Sally said, rubbing her eyes, sore from slicing so many onions.

'I didn't want to do anything too grand. Just some real, authentic, Indian street food. The sort of cooking that comes from the heart, rather than the sort of thing that would be served at the palace to look incredible but which might be a bit lacking in flavour,' Ameera said, completely at home at the stove.

'So these marinades you're making now, will you just leave these to soak into the meat until it's ready to cook on Thursday?' Mrs Mackle said.

'Exactly. The longer the better for everything to come together and really penetrate the meat,' said Ameera.

'And you haven't forgotten about the no-nuts rule? You wouldn't believe how many people react to them and how dangerous it can be!' Mrs Mackle said.

'Why, what would happen?' Sally asked, thinking how weird it was to be having a relatively normal conversation with Mackle the Jackal!

'Oh, you don't want to know. If you're allergic, even the tiniest speck of nut dust can make your throat swell up so much you can't breathe,' Mrs Mackle said, clutching her neck.

'Oh my goodness, that's awful. Is there anything anyone can do to reverse it once the symptoms start or do you just . . . well, die?' Sally asked, forgetting to be tactful.

'I'd say you'd be in serious trouble if there wasn't one of these nearby,' came a voice from the doorway. And there was Butch, present and massive as ever, walking towards them with his hand outstretched.

'This is an EpiPen. It contains an injection of adrenaline, which stops an allergic reaction very quickly and helps to reduce swelling,' Butch said, before replacing it in his suit breast pocket. I always carry one, as I also have a severe nut allergy, believe it or not.'

'See! I told you it's more common than you'd think. Places like schools and hospitals have to follow strict regulations about food content these days,' Mrs Mackle said. 'That's you and Mrs Fuller at L'Etoile, and that's just among the staff! There might be students here who don't even know if they're allergic yet.'

'Goodness me, Jai,' Ameera said. 'You never told me that!'

 Yes, Story-seeker, Butch has a name. It's Jai!

'I absolutely promise,' she went on, 'no nuts! It's been a nice challenge to perfect other flavours, to be honest. It's good for me to think of alternatives. I thought I'd make some samosas today too. The more we can do now, the less of a panic I'll be in on Thursday. Do we know who's judging yet?' Ameera asked.

'One of the girls' fathers, I think,' Mrs Mackle said, licking her lips at the sight of Ameera plating up some golden little parcels. 'He's a world-famous chef

– Italian apparently – I forget the name . . . '

'Oh you must mean Sofia's dad, Antonio Russo Vincenzi?' Sally said. 'I remember him donating an auction prize of tickets to his Michelin-starred restaurant in Venice.'

'Yes!' Mrs Mackle said. 'That's right, he's judging along with Mrs Fuller and Madame Ruby, of course!'

'Oh my goodness. *He's* Sofia's father? He's the best Italian chef in the world!' Ameera said. 'I loved that TV series he did about cooking in Sicily!'

'Wow! You do know about food!' Sally said, recalling her mum talking about that series when it had been on.

'Just a little,' Ameera said with a smile as she handed out the most delicious vegetable samosas anyone had ever tasted.

'Can we try some too?' Molly said, appearing at the kitchen door with Maria, Danya, Honey and Pippa in tow. 'We're starving!'

Mrs Mackle was in such raptures about the taste sensation she was experiencing, she'd have said yes to just about anything. 'Try the onion bhajis – they are the sweetest, crunchiest things I've ever tasted,' she said, dribbling onto her chin like a purring cat.

As the girls tucked into Ameera's culinary delights,

Molly snapped a few sneaky precious memories of the *chef princess* in her element.

'Princess, we ought to return to Garland. It's already very late and I fear Miss Coates will be on the war path,' Butch (aka Jai) said, with a glance at Mrs Mackle.

'Oh go on,' she said. 'You go. I'll clear up here. I'm the only one who does it properly anyway,' she said, thinking that after they'd gone, she could munch her way through the rest of the goodies.

'Oh thank you, Mrs Mackle. That's so kind. Help yourself to anything other than the onion pickle,' Ameera said. 'I'll need all of that for Thursday – oh and the marinade for the chicken thighs and lamb fillets just needs covering and popping in the fridge.'

'No problem. Good night, Your Highness. Good night, *Jai*,' Mrs Mackle said, blushing in Butch's direction.

'Tell me she wasn't flirting?' Maria whispered in genuine alarm as they scooted out of the Ivy Room.

'She was flirting . . . ' Pippa said.

'OMG I think I just threw up a bit in my mouth!' Maria said, looking decidedly pale.

'Gross!' Molly said.

And with that, seven full tummies took to their beds at the end of a very long but satisfying day!

11

A Dress Rehearsal

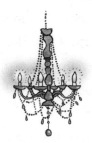

'How did you get on, Moll?' Maria asked as they exited their dreaded maths exam.

'I've no idea. Can't tell whether I just got it all a hundred per cent wrong or a hundred per cent right . . . that's how much I don't have a clue what I'm doing when it comes to algebra,' Molly said.

'But what about all the work we did at the weekend on it? I really thought you were starting to get your head around it,' Maria said.

'I know! It just doesn't stay in my head. Put it this way: if you'd asked me three years ago what algebra was, I'd have said a piece of underwear covered in seaweed!'

Sally giggled. 'I'll have to remember that one for my repertoire. Well, look on the bright side! The exams are officially over!'

'Oh my gosh, you're right! She's right! No more revision stress . . . and just in time for us to sing and dance ourselves to the end of term!' Molly said.

'Ameera – hey!' Sally called, seeing the princess coming towards them. 'How did you find it?'

'Not too bad – except I used Pi to work out the answer to the last question, and I don't think that was right at all.'

Danya couldn't help raising an eyebrow. She, like her fellow brainy buddy, Maria, found algebra the most logical and simple thing in the world.

'I knew it! I can't believe I got that wrong. How annoying! Too late to worry about it now. At least it's all over,' Ameera said. 'I wonder what Miss Joshi's plans are for us this afternoon. I could do with splitting my time between the Bolshoi rooms and the kitchen. I'm worried I've over-garlicked my lamb dish and wouldn't mind weakening the marinade a bit before cooking it tomorrow.'

'Let's go back to class and ask Miss Joshi what the plan is,' Molly said. 'I'm sure there'll be enough time for you to do both.'

'No need, I can tell you right now,' said Miss Joshi, coming up behind them.

'Wowsers, she's got bat ears!' Danya whispered to Maria, only to be shot an *I heard that!* look from Miss Joshi.

'The plan, girls, from now until the Extravaganza is rehearse, rehearse, rehearse!'

'Great.'

'Brilliant!'

'Wicked!' the responses echoed up and down the corridor.

Miss Joshi looked up and saw she had all her girls together. 'While you're here, I might as well tell you the good news,' and she turned to face Ameera. 'Your parents, Ameera, have confirmed that they will be attending the performance part of the Extravaganza tomorrow afternoon!'

'They are?' Ameera turned to Sally in surprise. To be honest, this whole term had been such a whirlwind for her, she'd barely had time to miss home, let alone spend much time on the phone to her parents. They were busy as usual and for once in her life, so was she. It was lovely that they were finally going to come and see her in action. Then she realised . . .

'Oh no! This means I can't cook, or perform! They wouldn't like it. Especially if they're actually going to be here to see it. They'll go crazy when they see how involved in everything I am,' Ameera said, looking at the floor to hide her tears.

Sally grabbed her arm. 'Oh, Ameera. Are you absolutely sure they'd object?'

'Positive! It's happened before at a school I went to in Paris. They didn't even make that performance but left strict instructions that I could be instrumental in the planning but not the execution . . . or something along those lines,' Ameera said.

'But then why did you agree to do the cooking, and the choreography, and the rest, if you knew it would get you into such trouble?' Molly said, feeling desperately sorry for the princess.

'I'm not sure. You guys gave me the courage I guess, but if my parents are turning up to sit in the audience I'm doomed!'

'I wouldn't be so sure about that, Ameera,' Miss Joshi said, having heard the tail end of the girls' conversation.

'Excuse me?' Ameera said, politely.

'I took the liberty of contacting Mrs Kapoor on your behalf, to request the permissions necessary for you to experience L'Etoile life to the full,' Miss Joshi began to explain.

'You did?' Ameera's eyes were like saucers . . . great big saucers of hope.

'Of course,' Miss Joshi began. 'My roots are in India too. I know how these things work and didn't want you to find yourself in a position of reproach.'

'What does she mean?' Honey whispered to Danya.

'She didn't want her to get in trouble!' Danya whispered back. 'Shh!'

' . . . and I'm delighted to say that your parents are happy, on this occasion, to allow you to enjoy the Extravaganza to the full and participate like any other student,' she concluded.

'Really?' Ameera said meekly. This was unbelievable news.

'Really. All it needed was a promise from Madame Ruby for there to be no press present and the temporary confiscation of anything that could be used as a camera in the theatre for staff, students and guests,' Miss Joshi said.

'And Madame Ruby agreed?' Maria said, thinking how unlike old Ruby that sounded. She'd always used any performance as a PR opportunity for the school and had the world's press on speed dial! Missing out on a chance to have the princess's name linked to L'Etoile must have been such a sacrifice. Still, at least

Ameera's parents would be there, and no doubt she would be at their side at *all* times.

'Oh thank you, so much!' Ameera said, smiling at her teacher. 'You've been so thoughtful. The fact that I can cook and dance . . .'

'And sing!' Pippa interrupted.

'Ha! Why not . . . yes, even sing . . . with all my friends, means the world to me.'

'Then what are you waiting for?' said Miss Joshi. 'I think a dress rehearsal is what's needed this afternoon, with the rest of the year. I'll check in with Three Beta to see if they're available. And I'd like to come and watch, if that's all right?'

'Absolutely!' came the response.

Within seconds the corridor was a ghost town. Fashion Faye and her helpers had gone back with Ameera and Butch to collect up the costumes, while the rest ran off to the Kodak Hall to see if there was any chance of grabbing the stage for a couple of hours.

'Didn't I tell you L'Etoile would change your life, Ameera?' Molly said.

'Yes, but I didn't believe you. I didn't think I could

do that *reach for the stars* stuff. Little did I know. It's just amazing!' Ameera said, giving Molly's hand a squeeze.

'Do you think it could mean a bit more freedom for you?' Maria said.

'I'm not sure, but if they'll just recognise my passion for cooking and let me loose in the kitchen, I'll be the happiest girl alive!'

Miss Joshi arrived with Three Beta, who were keen to put in some dress-rehearsal time.

'Ameera, did I hear that you will be singing tomorrow afternoon?' Miss Joshi asked.

'Yes!' Pippa and Maria said before Ameera had the chance to change her mind.

'She's brilliant!' Pippa said.

'Oh Pippa! Don't be silly. You're the singer. I'm just going to wail a bit!' Ameera said, blushing.

'Just wait and see,' Pippa told Miss Joshi.

'Princess, it does seem there is no end to your talents,' Miss Joshi said. 'How wonderful you've finally got this opportunity to shine.'

The girls were bubbling with excitement, admiring each other's luxurious costumes and perfecting all the dance steps Ameera had shown them. Molly and Honey had been practising henna tattoos all week and had effortlessly perfected the craft, with each girl sporting the most beautiful, personalised tattoo. Faye had a box of junk jewellery full of gold bangles, enough for everyone to snake up their arms and adorn their ankles. Once they were together on the stage in all their finery they really did look superb.

The routine opened with Pippa staring out of a window, her long hair tumbling around her like Rapunzel in the tower, watching the hustle and bustle of a busy street below – played by the rest of the third year. Pippa, watching from above, longed to join them. The music started slowly, Pippa's beautiful voice floating through the streets.

A bird with a dream,
To roam the world with others,
To soar the skies and reach for the stars,
Yearning for a life so free . . .

Then the spotlight turned on Ameera, who appeared in the shadows behind Pippa, acting the part of her conscience. As Pippa sang, Ameera's soft but purposeful voice urged her to stay in the tower. But Pippa climbed down to the street party. Then came an amazing modern Bollywood dance track, drowning Ameera's lilt completely, and everyone danced. The vibe was fun: free and pure. Ameera's voice cut in, louder across the dance track, pulling Pippa back to her tower. Finally the scene faded to black with Ameera's vocal closing the sequence.

Everyone clapped and cheered. It was a breathtaking performance. The colours of the costumes and precision of the choreography was magical, and the girls knew it.

'Simply marvellous!' Miss Joshi said. 'I'm impressed. It's very professional, girls. And the storyline ... what storytelling! A girl who longs for a life in the real world, but who's brought back to her ivory tower. Very interesting. Very interesting indeed. '

'Oh, you don't think it's too much?' Ameera said in a panic. Perhaps her story idea had been too obvious and would leave her exposed.

'Not at all. It's the first honest piece of theatre I've seen in a very long time and I praise all of you for your talent and maturity in handling it so beautifully. It will be the talk of the town, I assure you!' Miss Joshi said, turning away to talk to the Three Beta girls.

'She seemed to really like it!' said Danya.

'Let's hope Ameera's parents feel the same way,' Molly whispered to Honey.

'Come on, let's get these outfits off before I spill something on mine. I'd still like to work on that track some more. The end few bars could do with a bit of tinkering,' said Maria.

'No, please, Maria. I can't face any more studio time with you. I love you, but you are a dragon! Uncle Harry's got nothing on you!' Pippa exclaimed.

'Thank you! I'll take that as a compliment!'

'Maybe we could have a few more run-throughs? I'd feel more confident if we could. I didn't even know I'd be singing for sure until just now!' said Ameera.

'Sure!' Maria turned to the others. 'Let's go for a re-run, girls. From the top!'

'All good, Ameera?' Pippa said, feeling a little bit hoarse.

'Yes! Much better. Thanks, everyone. I appreciate you staying on to run through it a few more times. I'm proud to be performing with you. You're so talented!' Ameera said.

The whole room was beaming.

Suddenly there was a loud bang as the double doors at the back of the Kodak Hall flew open to reveal a stony-looking Madame Ruby marching towards them, followed closely by Mrs Fuller and someone else.

'Oh my gosh, it's Mrs Kapoor!' Ameera gasped. 'Something must be wrong!'

'I'll say,' Sally said. 'I haven't seen that face on Madame Ruby since L'Etoile was under attack from Lucifette's ghost last year!'

'Princess Ameera,' Madame Ruby said sternly. 'Would you come with us, please?'

Butch was at Ameera's side in a second. Ameera nodded to him that it was OK, but her face told a different story. She'd never felt so panicked. Mrs Kapoor hadn't ever arrived unannounced before. It must be something really bad!

'Are my parents all right?' she murmured.

'Yes, they're fine,' Mrs Kapoor said. 'Come. We need to speak privately.'

Sally took a protective step towards the trembling princess.

'Sally, would you come with me?' Ameera said.

'Of course,' Sally said.

'Princess, I don't think that would be appropriate

in the circumstances—' Mrs Kapoor began but was cut short.

'Mrs Kapoor. As yet I do not know to which circumstances you refer and until I do, I absolutely insist that Miss Sudbury accompany me,' Ameera said with an authority which only comes from being royal.

Wow, go Ameera, the girls thought.

Mrs Kapoor nodded, before ushering Ameera and Sally towards the doors.

Suddenly Maria dived into her bag, before running over to Sally and giving her the most enormous hug. To everyone watching, it was the most bizarre scene, but as soon as Sally felt something chunky slip into her pocket, she knew exactly what Maria was up to. *Clever Maria!*

The theatre exploded into a din of gossip.

'Oh my gosh, I wonder what's happened?' Belle said.

'I hope her parents haven't been in an accident or anything!' said Danya.

'You heard Mrs Kapoor, they're fine,' said Molly.

'Then what can it be? Must be something pretty

dire for Madame Ruby to call in the ambassador!'
Pippa said.

'And what was all that hugging about, Maria? That
was a bit weird!' Danya said.

'My thoughts exactly! What are you up to, Mimi?'
asked Molly.

Maria had a glint in her eye. 'Put it this way. I've
got a horrible feeling it's got something to do with the
faker! She has finally struck and we never even saw it
coming!'

'I think you might be right. This is all just too much
of a coincidence – something that affects Ameera,
twenty-four hours before our big show,' said Honey.

'We're not going to find out anything standing here.
Quick, back to the room. I have an idea!' Maria said
and the girls followed her back to Garland, leaving
the rest of the third year in a complete whirlwind of
confusion.

12

Revelations

'*I* know we say it all the time, but you are the fastest-thinking genius on planet earth!' Molly said, full of admiration for her sister who'd tipped out her famous gadget box all over the bedroom floor. As soon as Molly saw the charger Maria had selected and plugged into the socket, she knew exactly what that *Sally hug* had been about.

'Would someone tell me what's going on?' Honey said, completely at a loss.

'I have to admit, I can't think what you're up to either,' said Danya, feeling grumpy that she didn't understand Maria's plan.

'Tah-dah!' Maria said, holding out one of the girls'

faithful old adventure walkie-talkie watches.

'Ooh, that's a good idea!' Pippa said. 'But if we're going to eavesdrop on Madame Ruby's office, how are we going to get another one in there?'

'Tell me you didn't just happen to have a fully charged, turned on, walkie-talkie watch in your bag which you shoved into Sally's pocket just now!' Danya said in disbelief.

'Shh!' Maria said with a grin, as she scrolled through the channels trying to find which one Sally was on.

'There – stop!' Molly said, hearing Madame Ruby's voice telling Ameera to have a seat.

'Dan, can you record it on your phone in case we miss anything? Lucky for us it sounds like they're just getting started,' Maria said.

'Yes!' Danya said and the group huddled round to listen.

'Princess Ameera, we find ourselves in a very grave situation,' Madame Ruby began, clearly distressed.

Ameera couldn't even begin to imagine what she was about to say next.

'It's something which threatens not only your

reputation, but the reputation of L'Etoile itself as a safe haven for its staff and students. I presume you know what I'm referring to by now?'

Ameera looked blank.

'Just tell your side of the story, Princess Ameera,' Mrs Kapoor said. 'We only want to put this right and try to prevent a media storm.'

Sally looked at Ameera, only to see that she had no clue as to what Madame Ruby was referring to, any more than she had. She just prayed the walkie-talkie watch was working and that the girls were getting all this!

'Madame Ruby, Mrs Kapoor, Mrs Fuller. One of you is going to have to tell me what this is about as I've no idea,' Ameera said in her serious princess tone.

'Princess Ameera,' Mrs Kapoor stepped in. 'It appears that a journalist called Ben Bainley at the *London Gazette* has received an email containing a diary of your life here as a L'Etoilette and let's just say it doesn't paint either you, or the school in a very good light.'

Ameera looked horrified.

'And to add insult to injury, it contains some private and damaging information about your life as a princess which won't be looked on at all favourably by your parents,' Mrs Kapoor continued.

Madame Ruby nodded to Mrs Fuller, who handed

a blue document wallet to a very pale Ameera.

'Are these, or are these not, *your* words, Ameera?'

'Absolutely not!' Ameera said angrily, barely glancing at the papers before handing the folder back. 'I do not keep a diary, nor do I make a habit of contacting journalists!'

'But these are printed emails, sent from *your* email account,' Mrs Fuller explained. 'Let me see here, yes, your address . . . is it ameera@secureroyalnetwork. co.in?'

'Yes it is,' Ameera said, suddenly on alert.

'Let's have a look at these emails together, Ameera,' Sally said softly, feeling desperately sorry for her friend. 'Or we'll never get to the bottom of this.'

As Ameera started to read the first page, her eyes nearly popped out of her head. She flicked through the pages, pages of letters, addressed to *Dear Diary*.

Dear Diary,
I'd like to play a game of football, dressed in a Chelsea kit . . .

Dear Diary,
While I get to see the most incredible things as a princess, I rarely get to DO anything myself . . .

She didn't have to look far to realise she'd been betrayed. She'd never written those diary pages, but the thoughts and feelings were hers, in her words, from her emails to *Yours, L'Etoilette*. She read out loud, trying to make sense of it.

Dear Diary,
I'd like to do anything that feels like complete chaos . . . to cross the line . . .

Dear Diary,
I wish I was normal . . . there, I said it. I wish I was normal and not trapped by expectations of what is acceptable for a princess and what isn't . . .

'I don't understand,' Sally said, feeling trapped between a rock and a hard place. It had taken her and the Garland girls listening only seconds to realise that these diary excerpts had been used in a way Ameera had never intended by the fake *Yours, L'Etoilette*, but she could hardly say anything to Ameera and the others without unveiling Maria as the real *Yours, L'Etoilette*.

'Nor do I!' Tears were starting to trickle down Ameera's cheeks.

'What are you saying, Princess?' Mrs Kapoor asked, taking a seat behind her. 'That you didn't say these things or send this diary to the *London Gazette*?'

'What?' Ameera said, jumping out of her seat. 'No! I mean yes. I mean yes, they're my words . . . but *no* I don't keep a diary and *no* I didn't send anything to any newspaper!'

'Then how did these words, not to mention a file of very damaging photographs, end up in an email from you, via your email account, to the entertainment editor of the *London Gazette*?' Madame Ruby asked as calmly as she could.

Just when she thought things couldn't get any worse, Ameera heard the word *photograph* and gasped. *Photos!* She thought. *Of me?* Her breathing was fast and shallow.

Sally didn't know what to do for the best. *Come on, girls*, she thought. *We need you!*

Maria had gone into a meltdown as soon as she heard the mention of Chelsea football club. Ameera had only ever mentioned that in the one email that she'd sent her when Maria was trying to get to know her a bit and repair some of the damage the fake *Yours, L'Etoilette* had done.

'I thought you said you deleted that email straight away in case the faker hacked in and read it!' Danya said.

It was safe to say that the girls listening felt completely helpless and as if they'd utterly failed to protect their new friend from harm.

'I did, I did! I printed it as soon as we read it and then I deleted it!' Maria snapped.

'Well, the faker got hold of it somehow and is using it against Ameera,' Molly replied.

'Tell me you emptied the trash folder after you deleted it,' Pippa said. 'Remember that's how we caught the faker in the first place.'

Maria went pale. She must have done. She wouldn't have forgotten a simple thing like that, would she?

Her face said it all. There it was, clear as day: Ameera's email where she talked about longing to be normal, pillow fights and feeling trapped . . . in fact everything the faker had used to create the damaging diary.

'You didn't, Mimi . . . ' Molly said, her face falling.

'I'm sorry. Sometimes there's just so much running through my head I forget even the simplest of things,'

Maria said, her head in her hands. *How could I have been so stupid?*

'Guys . . . shh . . . they're showing Ameera the photos. She's talking again now,' Honey said, not having left the walkie-talkie for a second.

'You think I sent *these*?' Ameera said shakily. 'Why would I? This would be the end of life as I know it. I'll be banished to my room for eternity where I can bring no more shame to my family!'

Sally tightened her grip around Ameera's shoulder. As soon as she saw the first few photos she recoiled, realising they must have come from Honey and Molly's secret album. But how did the *Gazette* get them? The girls had those photo cards under lock and key in their bedroom! What should she say? If she helped Ameera and told the truth, she'd drop the others in it. Where, oh where were they with some lightning bolt of a rescue plan? There was nothing for it. She'd have to encourage Ameera to tell them about *Yours, L'Etoilette* . . . but without letting Ameera know that she knew about her emails to *Yours, L'Etoilette*. Could this get any more confusing? Talk about piggy in the middle!

'None of this makes any sense,' Sally said honestly. 'Let's go back to the beginning and think about it logically ... Ameera, you said the words are yours, and that you didn't send any email to the *Gazette*, which can only mean two things: either that someone's a mind-reader, or that you've been hacked,' Sally said boldly.

'Go, Sally!' Maria and Danya exclaimed, listening to Sally taking control of the situation.

'Yes, tell us what you meant, Princess. The truth, please,' Mrs Kapoor said.

'I said those things,' Ameera said, wiping her eyes. 'All of them, but not in the way they come across in those diary entries. They make me sound so ungrateful, so trapped. I didn't write them like that.'

'Go on, Ameera,' Sally said.

'I was chatting with the school blogger you put in touch with me before I arrived,' Ameera said.

'What blogger? I did no such thing,' Madame Ruby said, to Ameera's surprise.

'You didn't? Then who gave her my email address in the first place?'

'Gave *who* your email address? I don't know any bloggers,' Madame Ruby snapped.

'Do you mean *Yours, L'Etoilette*, Ameera?' Sally

said, trying to help things along. She still wasn't sure it was the right plan of action, but she had to do something.

'Yes,' Ameera said simply. 'I've been emailing her since before I arrived at L'Etoile. I thought she was my friend.'

Mrs Kapoor looked at Madame Ruby, and Madame Ruby looked at Mrs Fuller.

'I am aware of a student *agony aunt* type blogger,' Mrs Fuller said. 'It's my business to be aware of all student correspondence. I check the *Yours, L'Etoilette* site from time to time and have to say that until now, I've had no cause for concern. I've only ever found her to be informative and sensitive and until now would only praise the student behind this initiative. What are your thoughts, Sally? Have you had any personal experience with *Yours, L'Etoilette*?'

Here we go, Sally thought. *Poker face, Sally! Don't give anything away!* (Thoughts echoed across the quadrant by five very nervous Garland girls.)

'I have, actually, when I first arrived. *Yours, L'Etoilette* talked me out of more than one predicament. But I've only ever found her to be a real help,' Sally said honestly.

'This isn't getting us anywhere,' Madame Ruby

snapped. 'And it's not looking terribly good for you, Ameera. Your parents are already on their way here, to the very place that will shortly be a nest of press vipers if this story runs in the morning. Literally every news outlet worldwide will want to print your controversial *Diary of a Real-life Princess*, and the accompanying photos of you.

'Midnight feasts, pillow fights, water fights, fancy dress parties with your precious gowns . . . shall I go on?'

Ameera stared wide-eyed at Sally. One thing was clear, at least where the photos were concerned, and the Garland girls felt it too. Molly was mortified to discover that both the memory sticks from her camera and Honey's were missing from the keepsake box they'd been compiling for Ameera's leaving present.

'What can we do?' Sally said desperately. 'Ameera said she had nothing to do with any of this so what can we do to stop them from running the story?'

'The problem, Sally,' Mrs Kapoor said, 'is that as far as the *Gazette* are concerned, they have the proof they need to go to print. They have photographic evidence from your diary wish-list, Ameera, and I'm sorry to say that we're powerless to stop them.' She paused to think. 'If we were in India, your father might have been able to squash the story, but the British press is the hungriest in the world.'

Ameera went quiet. 'I know!' she jumped up. 'I've got proof too! Proof of the original emails I sent to *Yours, L'Etoilette*. They'll still be in my sent items. That will show you I'm not lying. I did say those things but not in the way they've been presented.'

Mrs Kapoor popped her head out of the door and dispatched Butch to get the princess's laptop.

'Yes, that's it! This is how we prove *Yours, L'Etoilette* is the one behind this and expose her for the misery she's caused!' Ameera said. Her tears had turned to anger and she was on a mission now. She wasn't sure who she trusted. Even Sally could be part of this. Some of those photos could only have been taken by someone who was there at the time. It had to be one of the girls . . . one of her girls. Ameera felt sick.

Sally didn't know which way to turn. She knew Ameera suspected her and the others of passing on those photos, and she was right! The look she'd given her had been one of pure heartbreak.

There was a knock at the door and Butch came in carrying a silver laptop.

'Set it up on my desk,' said Madame Ruby.

But before Butch could close the door behind him, a face appeared there.

'Maria!' Sally exclaimed. The cavalry had arrived! Finally!

'Not now, Maria,' Mrs Fuller said, uncertain whether Madame Ruby was about to blow a gasket. 'It's not a good time.'

'I know it's not, Mrs Fuller, but I need to speak to you and Madame Ruby in private. I wouldn't ask if it wasn't really important. It's about Ameera,' Maria said, her face flushed with nerves.

Ameera scowled at Maria, fearing her suspicions were correct.

'We'll talk next door in your office, Mrs Fuller,' Madame Ruby said. 'Ameera, you log on and see what you can come up with and we'll be back shortly.'

Maria followed them out of the head's office and closed Mrs Fuller's door behind her.

13

Maria's Theory

'This had better be good, Maria,' Madame Ruby said.

'Talk to us,' Mrs Fuller said, praying Maria wasn't about to get herself expelled.

Maria took a deep breath.

'I'm *Yours, L'Etoilette*,' she said quietly.

'I'm sorry,' Madame Ruby said sharply. 'I thought you just said that you are *Yours, L'Etoilette*, this elusive and, as it turns out, evil blogger!'

'I did,' Maria said again.

Mrs Fuller shook her head. 'Oh, Maria. Why can we never have a single crisis at L'Etoile without you and your friends being in it up to your necks?'

'Please,' Maria said calmly. 'If you'll just hear me out, you'll understand.'

Madame Ruby once again looked at Mrs Fuller and then sat down with a sigh.

'I'm *Yours, L'Etoilette*,' Maria began. 'Have been since the start. But she's not the evil blogger she's been made out to be today. Like you said, she's informative and sensitive . . . '

Mrs Fuller nodded, then wondered how Maria could possibly have known she'd said that when she hadn't even been in the room!

Maria winced, realising her mistake and quickly carried on to avoid any questions about eavesdropping. Within seconds, the whole story came tumbling out, starting from their arrival at school after the holidays: meeting Ameera, hearing that she'd been corresponding with *Yours, L'Etoilette* for advice about life at L'Etoile, knowing she'd not seen a single email from the princess and realising that she, Maria Fitzfoster, had been hacked. She told them how she'd found all the emails in the deleted items folder but didn't feel the need to report it as there hadn't been any more since, only one that she, the real *Yours, L'Etoilette*, had sent to try to put the princess at ease and get to know her.

'So you're saying there's a fake *Yours, L'Etoilette* at the school, who took your identity solely for the purpose of tricking the princess into sharing her most private thoughts?' Mrs Fuller said.

'I realise that not reporting it was my biggest failure. If only I'd told you right away, all of this could have been prevented!' Maria said, feeling close to tears.

'Maria, the photos. Do you know who took them? It has to be one of the girls who were present. The pillow fight was in your room, for instance,' Mrs Fuller said, her voice full of disappointment.

'I can explain,' Maria said, gathering herself.

'But you know not a single photograph of the princess is permitted to be taken without prior authority! I thought I made that quite clear at the start of term!' Madame Ruby said, exasperated.

'I know, but they were supposed to be a gift,' said Maria.

'A gift! To whom? The world's press?' Madame Ruby just about shouted.

'No . . . no! The gift was Molly and Honey's idea and we agreed it was a lovely one. They've been secretly taking photos to make a memory book for her. She seemed so sad when she arrived so we thought it would be nice to try to create some experiences for her

– like the pillow fight and even the water fight . . . ' she trailed off.

'We were going to give Ameera all the printed photos and the memory sticks too so she wouldn't have to worry about anything falling into the wrong hands, but it seems our room was raided and they were taken. We really are sorry.'

Madame Ruby and Mrs Fuller were thoughtful.

'So if Ameera didn't send that email to the *Gazette* and you, as the mysterious *Yours, L'Etoilette*, didn't either, then who has hacked you both?' asked Mrs Fuller.

'And why? Apart from ruining the princess's reputation and that of my school. What could any student possibly have to gain by that?' Madame Ruby said.

'I'm not entirely sure it is one of the girls,' Maria said. Madame Ruby and Mrs Fuller looked at her intently.

'You said it yourself. Ameera's the target. She's told us, on more than one occasion, that there are members of her family who don't believe in her place among them,' Maria explained.

'Why would they think such a thing?' Madame Ruby said, horrified.

'Because she's adopted,' said Mrs Fuller, instantly realising what Maria was getting at.

'Exactly!' said Maria. 'If Ameera could be publicly

shamed by her actions, those family members could use it against her.'

'And stake their claim to her inheritance!' Mrs Fuller said.

'Bingo!' Maria said, thinking how even more amazing this all sounded now that she was saying it out loud.

'That's quite an accusation, Maria,' Madame Ruby said.

'There's no other explanation. No other student at L'Etoile would know how to hack me, let alone Princess Ameera.'

'But no one except me, Mrs Fuller and Mrs Kapoor knew Ameera was coming to L'Etoile. It wasn't reported in the press so it must be someone at the school, and I refuse to believe it could be any of my staff or students – so who, exactly, are you suggesting it might be, Maria?' Madame Ruby asked.

'I don't know for sure,' Maria said.

'But you have a shortlist of suspects?' said Mrs Fuller.

'I do!' Maria said. Suspect *singular*, really. It has to be someone who's been close to us at all times; someone who knows what we've been up to; someone who would have the stealth to break into our room to steal a memory card; and the skills to hack into our email accounts. Who better than the head of Ameera's secret service – Butch?' Maria said, forgetting that was only his nickname.

'Butch? Why do I feel as if I'm in a movie? Who is *Butch*?' Madame Ruby said in dismay.

'I think Maria's referring to Jai, Ameera's head of security,' Mrs Fuller said, the cogs starting to turn in her own mind. Of course! It would make perfect sense for it to be him. He has the skill set and the connections to make it possible, but Maria, are you sure? He seems so loyal to Ameera.'

Maria's phone beeped.

'May I?' she asked, thinking any text arriving at this moment must be important.

Madame Ruby rolled her eyes and poured herself a glass of water. Hackers ... secret service conspiracies ... and now students brazenly answering illegal phones right in front of her. *Whatever next?*

'It's Sally. She said the princess's sent items have been deleted so she's no proof whatsoever of her original emails to *Yours, L'Etoilette*. Butch has beaten us to it!

'He must have done it when I sent him to retrieve the princess's laptop!' Mrs Fuller said in despair.

'And I bet if I log on to my *Yours, L'Etoilette* email

account, he'll have emptied that too.'

'I can't believe it. That was our only hope of stalling the *Gazette*, once we realised the princess wasn't behind the whole thing herself,' Mrs Fuller said.

'Oh my goodness. What am I going to tell Ameera's parents when they arrive?' Madame Ruby wailed. 'It'll probably be splashed over every newspaper and news channel so they'll see it the minute they step off the plane!'

Maria was shocked to see Madame Ruby so panicky. She always seemed so in control, but here she was falling apart before Maria's eyes and it was unbearable.

'L'Etoile is finished! The school will be blacklisted by everyone from here to New Zealand! Discretion and exclusivity are paramount and without them, L'Etoile will never again be considered a safe environment.'

'You know, there might be a way,' Maria said suddenly, her mind in overdrive. 'Would you mind if I try?'

'You?' Madame Ruby said. 'What possible influence might you have at the *Gazette*?'

'Oh, you'd be surprised!' Maria put her phone to her ear and listened to it ring.

Gosh this girl was good, wasn't she Story-seeker? Talk about saving the day! What was she even doing at school anyway? She should be head of her own task force at Scotland Yard by now!

'Oh, hello. LT?' Maria said, watching as her headmistress's and deputy headmistress's mouths dropped open in surprise on hearing the familiarity with which Maria addressed the great Luscious Tangerella, editor of the *Gazette*.

Those of you who remember, Story-seeker, will know how Maria had impressed Luscious Tangerella so much with the exclusives she'd given the Gazette about their various adventures. As a result of her hard work as a budding investigative journalist, Maria had LT's trust and her own personal hotline to her hero.

'Yes, it's Maria . . . I'm sorry to bother . . . what? You were? Well, here I am, but would you mind if I start? I think I might have a scoop on that story you're working on about L'Etoile!' she paused, smiling at LT's excited response.

Mrs Fuller felt as if she might explode with pride.

'Yes, not only do I have the truth behind the *alleged* Princess Ameera emails but potentially a much bigger story for you – a royal conspiracy, you might say . . . yes . . . how long can you give me?' she asked, stopping to listen again.

Maria mouthed 'five p.m. tomorrow' at the two ladies staring at her. Mrs Fuller looked nervous.

'Wow. That doesn't give us long . . . yes, OK . . . I understand. So we have your word that Ben Bainley won't run anything until we've presented you with all the evidence tomorrow . . . right? OK, great. Speak to you then. Thanks so much, LT. I won't let you down!'

Maria hung up. That call couldn't have gone any better.

'Maria, you never cease to amaze!' Mrs Fuller said.

'Thank you. We've got less than twenty-four hours to disprove their story. Luckily for us LT's always hungry for something bigger and better, so we'd better piece something together and fast!'

'Madame Ruby,' Mrs Fuller said. 'Why don't you go back to your office and talk to Mrs Kapoor? Whatever happens here today, we need to know we have her onside. Then Maria and I will start digging up everything we can find on Jai. The more I think about it, the more I agree it can only be him – unless it's someone working remotely from India . . . but they would have to have someone on the inside. You can't break into someone's room and steal a memory card from India!'

'Absolutely,' Madame Ruby said.

'Um, sorry, Madame Ruby . . . one more thing,' said Maria. 'I don't think we should tell Ameera about me being *Yours, L'Etoilette*, or our suspicions about Butch yet. She's gone through quite enough without us making it worse. If she suspects I'm the one who's done this to her, I can't say how she'll react. Can we wait until we've got some real answers for her?'

'Fine,' Madame Ruby nodded. 'The less drama the better!'

'I half agree with that,' Mrs Fuller said thoughtfully. 'But I do think that we should leak the fact that we've managed to squash the story – even though we haven't quite yet. If the faker, assuming it is Butch, thinks that his plan has been scuppered, he might get careless and try something rash to get the same result – but this time we'll be ready for him!'

'Ooh! Good one, Mrs Fuller!' said Maria.

'Thank you!' Mrs Fuller said, rather pleased with herself.

'Do you think I can send for Danya Sawyer, please? She's an absolute genius when it comes to internet research and if I'm not mistaken, has probably already built up quite a file on Butch by now,' Maria said, pulling out her walkie-talkie watch – which thankfully was still switched on.

'Dan, girls. Receiving? Found anything on Butch yet? Over,' Maria said.

'Receiving, Mimi!' came Molly's voice through the watch. 'You were brilliant! Dan's already on her way to you! Over.'

Madame Ruby couldn't take any more surprises and left.

'I suppose Sally's got one of those in her pocket too?' Mrs Fuller said, shaking her head. 'Which is how you were able to quote me word for word and knew about the *Gazette* before you even entered the room!'

Maria smiled guiltily at her favourite teacher.

'OK. Thanks, guys. Back to you with the plan soon! Sit tight. Over!' Maria said and before she'd even put the watch down, there was a knock at the door and Danya entered sheepishly, carrying her laptop.

'Are we in terrible trouble?' she asked.

'That all depends . . . ' Mrs Fuller answered. 'On whether you girls can save the day again!'

The two girls winked at each other and set to work.

'You wanted to see me, Mrs Fuller?' Miss Joshi said, coming in to the office a little later.

'Yes – thank you for coming, Miss Joshi. I wondered if I might ask you to keep a close eye on the princess this afternoon.'

Miss Joshi was surprised to see two of her girls working earnestly in the deputy head's office.

'Why of course! Whatever's the matter?' she asked. 'Girls, I hope you haven't let yourselves or me down.'

Mrs Fuller suddenly realised how bizarre it looked. 'Oh my goodness, not at all, Miss Joshi. In fact, Maria and Danya are complete life-savers. They've been no end of help to me today.'

She turned to Miss Joshi to whisper more privately. 'The fact is, we're having a bit of a press issue regarding the princess, which is why I'd like you to keep an eye on her. She's very upset.'

'Of course. Anything I can do to help,' Miss Joshi said before disappearing next door to collect Ameera.

Meanwhile back in Madame Ruby's office, things had gone from bad to worse. On discovering that all of her sent items had been deleted, Ameera was sobbing her heart out on Sally's shoulder, about how she'd let everyone down. It was all Miss Joshi could do to keep up with the tissue requirement.

'Ameera, I do have a little good news,' Madame Ruby said, handing Mrs Kapoor a steaming cup of green tea. 'Thanks to my and L'Etoile's excellent relationship with the British press, I've just spent the last half an hour on the phone to the editor of the paper and am pleased to say that they have agreed to hold the story for now.'

'Oh, Madame Ruby!' Ameera looked up, her big brown eyes red and puffy. 'However did you manage it?'

'Yes. How did you?' Sally said cheekily, suspecting that Maria had been at the bottom of this little miracle.

'It will cost the school a much bigger story in return but luckily there's something I've been working on for a while. It just means I'll have to give an exclusive a bit faster than I'd hoped,' Madame Ruby continued, lying through her teeth.

No one dared ask about this mysterious exclusive.

'There, you see, Princess?' Mrs Kapoor said. 'I told you everything would work out.'

'You did and I thank you for your support,' Ameera said, blowing her bunged up nose as royally as she could. 'I don't think I would have ever recovered from the damage a story like that would have done to me and my parents.'

'Hopefully, they'll never have to know!' said Mrs Kapoor.

'Goodness me, it's nearly the end of supper. Why don't you girls go on?' Madame Ruby said. 'Miss Joshi, would you accompany them and try to calm the rumour mill? Perhaps just say our reasons for summoning the princess had something to do with her parents' imminent arrival.'

'Yes, of course,' Miss Joshi said, beckoning to Ameera and Sally to stand.

'But you'll find out who did this to me, won't you?' Ameera said suddenly, realising that just because the storm had temporarily passed, there was still the question of who that nasty *Yours, L'Etoilette* was, how she'd got all those photos and why she'd want to ruin her life like that.

'Without question!' Madame Ruby said. 'My people are working on it. Now you're not to worry any more about it, Ameera. When I have news, I'll come and find you.'

Ameera smiled for the first time in hours and turned to follow Miss Joshi down the hall.

Sally, who looked more confused than ever, just

stared at Madame Ruby, unable to understand anything that had just happened. *What had Maria told them? Had she even told them she was Yours, L'Etoilette?*

Seeing Sally in turmoil and immediately realising she must know more than she was letting on, Madame Ruby did something completely out of character and shot Sally the biggest wink and smile.

Wow! Sally thought. *Maria must have added hypnotism to her skills. She even had old Ruby dancing to her tune now. What a day!*

14

Busted!

While Ameera and Sally were left to fend off gossip in the Ivy Room, things were hotting up in Mrs Fuller's office. Three pairs of hands were furiously tapping away on laptops, looking for anything and everything they could find on *Big Bad Butch*.

'Anything?' Maria asked anxiously, starting to think that Butch more than deserved all the medals he wore with pride in the pictures.

'No!' Danya cried with frustration. 'He's a saint according to every article that mentions his name. 'He's been with the family since before Ameera was born and worked for the old prince before that!'

'Yes, but remember, that's just how undercover

spies work. They infiltrate and integrate themselves into their target's lives for years before they make their move – just to make doubly sure they don't fall under suspicion and get busted!' Maria said.

She sat back in her chair, frustrated.

We must be missing something. Think, Mimi, think! she told herself.

'I know!' Danya said suddenly. 'Maybe we're looking at this wrongly. Instead of focusing on Butch, maybe we need to try to connect him with the one person in India Ameera said wants her out of the way.'

Maria's eyes widened. 'Ooh, Danya . . . you little beauty. See, Mrs Fuller! I told you she was the best digger on planet internet!'

'It would help if we knew his name!' Danya said, her fingers working away on the keyboard again.

'Who?' Mrs Fuller said.

'HER UNCLE!' Danya and Maria said at once.

'Sorry . . . her uncle,' explained Maria. 'Ameera said he's always had an issue with her.'

'Probably because if Ameera hadn't been adopted, her uncle and his children would have inherited his brother's wealth,' Mrs Fuller said.

'Got him . . . Prince Abdul . . . I'm going into Google images first. We'll spot Butch's face in a photo far quicker than his name in an article,' said Danya, scrolling down.

Mrs Fuller and Maria crouched around the screen, each one scanning every image for a glimpse of the uncle and the security guard scheming together.

Suddenly Danya gasped, pointing at the screen. There were about nine shots visible, all of groups of different people with Prince Abdul.

'What is it, Dan?' Maria asked. 'I don't see him! Zoom in!'

Danya double-clicked onto an image of Prince Abdul in a fishing boat, proudly holding up a large catch, surrounded by half a dozen people.

One second later, Maria's hand flew to her mouth ... shortly followed by Mrs Fuller doing the same.

'Busted!' Danya said triumphantly.

15

To Trust or Not to Trust

Molly, Honey and Pippa couldn't wait for Sally, Danya and Maria to get back to the room. They'd seen Miss Joshi accompany Sally and Ameera into the Ivy Room for supper but hadn't dared speak to them. The suspense was killing them.

'Mimi!' Molly squealed as her sister and Danya finally walked through the door.

'What's happening? We heard it all – did you find anything on Butch? I can't believe it's him!' Pippa said.

'We'll tell you everything later, girls, I promise. But first we need to get Ameera back onside,' Maria said. 'Where's Sally?'

'Still with Ameera, I guess,' Molly said. They left

the Ivy Room before we did so they're probably in her room.'

'Good!' said Danya. 'Honey, where's the memory book?'

Molly pulled it out from under her pillow. 'Here it is. It's nowhere near finished though – not that it ever will be now that our memory cards have been stolen. The only photos in there are what we printed up before the weekend.'

'That will do,' Danya said.

'What are you going to do?' Pippa asked.

'We need to take it to Ameera now and explain that it was us who took the photos. We'll explain why, and that the memory cards were stolen, which is how they got to the press,' said Maria.

'And will you tell her you're *Yours, L'Etoilette*? *OMG, WFIN*!' Molly said to Maria, overcome with worry.

 OMG = Oh my goodness, Story-seeker, and *WFIN* = We're for it now!)

'Not just yet, sis,' Maria said. 'This will be enough for her to digest for the moment. We just need to win back her trust. She needs us now more than ever!'

'Do you think she'll believe us?' Honey said.

'She's going to have to!' Danya answered.

'But how will we get down the corridor to her room without Butch stopping us? He'll be on red alert trying to trip Ameera up, now he knows the story's not going to print!' Pippa said.

'That, Molly, my little actress extraordinaire, is where your skills come in!' Maria said, whispering something in Molly's ear.

Within seconds, Molly was skipping down the corridor in the opposite direction from Ameera's room.

Suddenly there was an almighty crash followed by the smashing of china.

Pippa popped her head out of the door and saw Butch running to Molly's aid – she'd accidentally on purpose crashed into the hall stand, bringing the whole thing down on top of her, including an entire vase of flowers complete with stinky water.

'Superstar!' Honey whispered.

'Go! Go! Go!' said Maria, and in a flash, the girls were inside Ameera's room, having texted Sally to open the door as soon as she heard *the sign*.

 Well, she couldn't very well have missed a sign like that, could she, Story-seeker!

It took some coaxing to get Ameera to listen to what her so-called *friends* had to say but finally she sat down and within seconds of looking through the most beautiful album of photos and messages, she couldn't not believe their story.

'It's so sweet that you would do this for me, girls,' she said, tearfully. 'It's so thoughtful.'

'That's just what we hoped you'd think,' Honey said. 'Not this nightmare we've ended up with.'

'We're sorry those memory cards got into the wrong hands. We just wanted you to have something to remember your time here by,' Pippa said.

'Oh, it's not your fault. It's that evil *Yours, L'Etoilette* who's behind all this,' Ameera said angrily. 'But don't worry – Madame Ruby is on it. They'll be found out and punished in no time.'

'I'm sure they will,' Maria said, and she meant it.

'We'd best get to bed. We've got a big day ahead tomorrow, or had you forgotten with everything else that's gone on this afternoon?' said Pippa.

'I know, we were just saying that before you guys arrived,' Sally said, standing up. 'Will you be all right, Ameera? Do you want me to stay with you tonight?'

'No, I'll be fine, Sally. Thanks for everything. You've been the best support a princess away from home could wish for.' Sally blushed.

As she turned to go, Sally spotted a little white envelope that had been pushed under the door.

'Looks like someone's sent you a message, Ameera,' she said, passing it to her.

'I wonder if it's from Madame Ruby! Will you read it out loud, Sally? My eyes are burning from all this crying!'

Maria and Danya were on their feet, immediately suspicious.

> *Dear Princess Ameera,*
>
> *I know who's behind this but I must meet you in person. If you want to know the truth, meet me in the Ivy Room tomorrow at 10 a.m. sharp, just before the judges arrive to adjudicate the bake-off, and I'll tell you everything then. It's not what you think. I know you have a busy morning tomorrow so I've tried to think of somewhere you need to be anyway.*
>
> *Yours, L'Etoilette*

Maria shot up and opened the door. The corridor was empty. Not even Butch was there. Probably with poor Molly, who was being checked over by Nurse Payne.

The room was silent.

'What do I do?' Ameera said nervously.

'I know it's a big ask given what's happened, Ameera, but do you trust us?' Maria said calmly.

The princess looked at the girls' kind faces and then at the beautiful memory book on her lap.

'Yes,' she said.

'Then do exactly as I tell you, and we'll get this trouble-maker.'

'OK, Maria,' Ameera said. She was all ears.

16

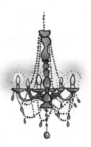

The Scene is Set

*A*fter what felt like hours of being monitored by Nurse Payne for Molly, and a sleepless night for the others as they wondered what was about to happen, the day of the international-bake-off-come-dance-Extravaganza dawned.

The Kodak Hall had been draped with flags from every nation and the Ivy Room looked and smelled ... good enough to eat! Mackle the Jackal and her army had worked through the night to set it up like a mini food festival with stalls from different countries at every turn.

The first years had chosen France and were serving Coq au Vin and Tarte Tatin for dessert. The second years had chosen Italy and their menu was a tasting board of mini pizzas, homemade tortellini with spinach and ricotta and tiramisu to follow. The third years had of course chosen India with an Indian street food menu, and the fourth and fifth years, China and England respectively. The Ivy Room was truly heaven for anyone with a love of cookery, or just eating!

Ameera and the chefs from the other years had been preparing and presenting their dishes since the crack of dawn until, at 9.30 a.m., Mrs Mackle announced the closure of the competition by clanging the biggest saucepan with the biggest ladle she could find.

Sally, who hadn't left Ameera's side, took her last spoonful of the most delicious curry she'd ever tasted.

'If you don't win this today, I'll never eat a curry again in protest!' she said, putting her arm around the princess.

'Thanks, Sally!' Ameera said. 'Though it's a wonder I managed to cook a single dish. My brain is fried with *what if* scenarios.'

'Look, we've got about twenty-five minutes before you have to be back here to meet *you know who*, so shall we go back to Garland for a quick chill out before the fun starts?'

'Yes, let's. Looks like everyone's gone back to get

changed for the judging now. Even Mrs Mackle's disappeared,' said Ameera.

'Thank goodness. I was worried you wouldn't have any bhajis left to be judged, at the rate she was scoffing them!' Sally giggled.

'That's why I made a double batch!' said Ameera. 'Can I come back to your room, Sally? I can't face being on my own at the moment.'

'Of course you can! Are you kidding? That'll give Molly and Honey the opportunity to give you the world's quickest makeover. They'll be happy!' Sally answered and, seeing Butch on the move, grabbed Ameera's hand and yanked her out of sight in an attempt to lose him.

It was the first time the girls had been together in daylight since the finger of suspicion had been lifted, and as Molly and Honey fussed around Ameera with their straighteners and lip-gloss, Danya decided now would be the perfect time to give Ameera another gift they'd been planning.

'Here you go,' Danya said. 'A little something from all of us.'

'What? Another present? For me?' Ameera said with a smile. 'But you've already given and done so much for me!'

'It's not much – but it means that you're going to have to come and visit us in the holidays!' Danya said.

Ameera's eyes lit up before she'd even opened the envelope. She'd dreamed of visiting friends and here they were. Seconds later she was staring at the most perfect blue and white crested pack and as she lifted the cover, seven tickets fluttered to the floor.

Ameera squealed with delight.

'It's to see the London derby in December at Stamford Bridge . . . Chelsea v Arsenal!' Sally said excitedly.

'Oh and you have to wear this!' Pippa said, pulling out a blue and white Chelsea football shirt with Ameera's name on the back. The princess's eyes shone with happiness.

'In fact, we all do!' Honey said, holding up six more shirts with TEAM AMEERA written on the back.

Ameera was in tears. How could she have doubted these wonderful, wonderful girls?

'I can't believe it! But how did you know my Chelsea secret?' Ameera asked, suddenly confused. She'd never said that out loud, she was sure of it.

Maria took a deep breath.

'I'm *Yours, L'Etoilette*,' she said quietly.

'What?' Ameera hissed, her whole demeanour changing.

'Don't panic!' Sally said. 'She's not the mean one, the one who sent you the note last night . . . she's the real one – the good one!'

'Ameera, we know you're confused,' Maria said. 'It's no wonder. I promise it will all become clear. I'm the real *Yours, L'Etoilette* but someone hacked me, the way they hacked you and wrote to the *Gazette* as you. Please, you have to trust us. Just for a little bit longer. OK?' She wondered whether she'd said too much.

Ameera took a deep breath and then smiled. 'I trust you,' she said. What choice did she have? If she didn't have the girls, she had no one. 'I trust you,' she said again. 'With you all at my side, I'm ready to face the world and whatever it throws at me today.' Tears started to prick her eyes again.

'That's our girl!' Maria said, hugely relieved. 'But before you go off and conquer the world, let's go catch ourselves a faker!'

17

To Catch A Traitor

As the Ivy Room clock struck ten, Ameera stood alone behind her food stall, waiting nervously. She just hoped the girls were still hiding behind the other stalls as they'd promised, poised and ready to rescue her if she needed it

As the minutes ticked by, she began to wonder if the fake *Yours, L'Etoilette* was ever going to show. Five past . . . ten past . . . quarter past ten. The judges would arrive soon. She picked up the large wooden spoon lying next to her curry and gave it a stir, adding a little more seasoning as she did so.

'Do you think Butch has bottled it?' Honey whispered to Molly.

As Ameera shook a little more salt into her lamb curry, the double doors swung open and Mrs Mackle waltzed in, followed by Madame Ruby, Mrs Fuller, Mrs Kapoor, Miss Joshi, and the great chef Antonio Russo Vincenzi.

Madame Ruby was extremely jovial. 'Now, Mr Russo, can I count on you not to unfairly favour the Italian cuisine?' she joked.

'But of course, Signora. I am offended you should even make such a joke!' he said playfully.

Ameera was frozen to the spot. How could *Yours, L'Etoilette* not even have turned up? And now there she was, somewhere she wasn't supposed to be, getting busted by the very people there to judge her cooking! Could this get any worse?

'Princess!' Mrs Mackle boomed. 'What are you doing here? You know you shouldn't be here now.'

Miss Joshi ran forward. 'Ameera. You should be waiting with the other chefs. Let me accompany you. It's just this—' She froze, a horrified look on her face. 'Ameera! What is the meaning of this? Are you trying to poison the school?'

Once again, Ameera looked confused. 'It's just a bit of salt. Sorry, I shouldn't be here. You're quite right, I—'

'Not that!' Miss Joshi shouted. 'This!' She leaned

♥ *169* ♥

forward to retrieve a large plastic jar and held it aloft.

'Ground almonds!' Mrs Mackle squealed. 'No nuts! No nuts!'

Mrs Fuller gasped and jumped backwards as only someone with a nut allergy would.

Ameera dropped her spoon, which clattered to the floor. 'No, honestly! I didn't . . . I haven't . . . it's not mine . . . ' she stammered.

'And I suppose you haven't contaminated the other dishes with it either?' Miss Joshi said.

Mrs Mackle was on the move, her beady eyes examining the other stalls.

'It will all have to go! Too dangerous! Too dangerous by far. It's impossible to tell if the other dishes have been tampered with. How could you, Princess?' she cried.

'Madame Ruby, I don't know what to say,' Miss Joshi said, turning to the judging group. 'Perhaps the no-nuts instruction was lost in translation. I take full responsibility for her behaviour. I should have done more—'

'Oh, you've done quite enough!' came a voice from the back of the room.

'Jai?' Ameera said, looking behind her, knowing that voice anywhere.

'He's here! What a nerve!' Molly whispered to Honey.

This was too much excitement for the girls crouching behind the food stalls and they immediately stood up for a better view.

'He's for it now – watch this!' Pippa said to Danya, who looked surprisingly unsurprised.

'What in heaven's name is going on?' asked Chef Russo, completely baffled.

'Please excuse us, Chef Russo, but it appears we have a traitor in our midst,' Madame Ruby explained. 'Someone present here this morning is out to destroy the reputation of our school and of Princess Ameera. Please forgive my keeping you in the dark but this matter is so serious, the culprit had to be caught in the act, in order for us to gain the proof we needed.'

'I see. Please, do go on,' Chef Russo said, intrigued.

By this time Jai had reached the group, holding a small video camera.

'I'm afraid, Miss Joshi, you have been caught red-handed, attempting to frame Princess Ameera,' he said as a gasp went up around the room.

'Joshi? No way!' Sally whispered to Pippa.

'This is better than the telly!' Honey said.

Maria and Danya merely winked at each other.

'What are you talking about?' Miss Joshi snapped, only to fall silent as the rest of the group watched the replay of the video of her entering the Ivy Room just before ten, shaking the contents of the ground almond jar into every dish in the room and then planting it at Ameera's stall.

'You're the faker?' Princess Ameera stammered. 'You did this? But why?'

'Forgive me, Princess. I should have recognised her sooner,' Jai said, his voice low and threatening. 'The imposter is Bula Chennai, an ex-student of mine from many moons ago. An excellent student but with questionable loyalty.'

'Oh my goodness, they know each other!' Maria whispered to Danya.

Miss Joshi looked like a naughty child cowering in front of her headmaster. She didn't say a word.

'How many years ago was it since you graduated from my security academy in Delhi? Must be at least fifteen,' Jai said.

'Seventeen years,' Miss Joshi said, her eyes fixed firmly to the floor.

'Quite an image change from the short-haired tomboy I trained back then. Tell me, how much is Prince Abdul paying you for this?' Jai said, angry that someone he'd taught had used his training against him and those he was sworn to protect.

'More than you ever would have!' Miss Joshi spat.

'Such a shame. Such a wasted talent, Bula. With this footage of you threatening the lives of anyone with a nut allergy today – myself included, and the contents of your laptop proving that you hacked into the princess's email and contacted the *Gazette*, I've enough evidence to put you away for a very long time. And I'm sure Prince Imran will be only too interested in your relationship with his brother.'

The room was silent, taking in what was unfolding before their eyes.

Miss Joshi opened her mouth to speak, only to be shot down by the ambassador.

'Save it for the judge, Miss Josh— Miss Chennai! The princess has already been through more than she ever should have this term. Get this criminal out of my sight, Jai. There's an embassy security vehicle ready to take her away.'

Jai nodded, then turned to Ameera.

'I'm so sorry, Princess Ameera. I'm afraid I almost failed you. I am most grateful for the intelligence and resourcefulness of your friends, and Madame Ruby and her staff,' he said.

'She had us all fooled, Jai. My unwavering faith in you remains.'

Molly, Maria, Pippa, Sally, Danya and Honey raced over to the Indian stall and enveloped Ameera in the biggest group hug they'd ever had.

'Thank you so much, girls. However did you work it all out?' Ameera asked.

'We had it all wrong to begin with! We thought it was Butch . . . sorry . . . Jai!' said Maria.

'Until we found a picture of Miss Joshi and your uncle on a fishing trip. It was too much of a coincidence to ignore!' Danya said.

'That's when we got Jai involved, and he very quickly put two and two together and made four,' added Maria.

'Excellent teamwork!' Mrs Fuller said. 'Now girls, I know you've been on a bit of a roller-coaster yet again this morning, but given that the cookery contest is now null and void, I think it best you go back to Garland and prepare for this afternoon's show.'

Ameera suddenly put her hand up to her mouth in a panic. 'But my parents! I bet Miss Joshi made up that part about getting permission for me to be in today's show – just to get me into even more trouble!'

'Oh my gosh, she's right,' Maria said.

'Actually,' Mrs Kapoor said, 'I obtained permission for you from your parents, but at the request of Mrs

Fuller, not Miss Joshi.'

Ameera smiled at Mrs Fuller. 'How did you even know to ask?'

'Princess, I make it my business to dot the "i"s and cross the "t"s half a dozen times where my L'Etoile students are concerned. Madame Ruby and I pride ourselves on our attention to detail.'

'Thank you so much,' Ameera said, gratefully.

'And on that note, you had better go and get ready,' Madame Ruby said. 'Signor Vincenzi, I can't apologise enough for wasting your time this morning. We couldn't have predicted that the traitor would ruin every dish in the bake-off. How can we make it up to you?'

'Madame, I feel like Poirot! It's been an honour to be part of your sting operation!' he said. 'I'd like to go and see my Sofia, now, if you don't mind.'

'Absolutely,' Madame Ruby said, shaking his hand warmly.

'We'll take you!' Honey said. 'We're going that way anyway.'

'Excellent!' said Madame Ruby, before turning to Mrs Mackle and Mrs Fuller to discuss what the other student chefs would be told as to why the bake-off had been ruined.

'Can I just ask what time my parents will be arriving?' Ameera said, suddenly longing to see them.

'Last word was that they will arrive just in time for the curtain up at two p.m. You girls will be closing the show so even if they're a bit late, they'll get to see your performance,' Mrs Fuller said.

'We're headlining?' Pippa exclaimed.

'Wicked!'

'Yessss!'

'Amazing!' the others exploded and ran off back to Garland, Chef Vincenzi bumbling behind them.

18

And They All Lived
Happily Ever After . . .

*Y*ou could have heard a pin drop as the spotlight faded on Ameera's face as the third years' performance came to an end.

'Hurrah!'

'Bravo!'

'Superb!' came the explosive reaction from an audience of parents, staff and students in the Kodak Hall.

Ameera had never experienced anything like it. The atmosphere was electric and there she was, not sitting on the sideline as usual, imagining what it might feel like to be centre stage, but actually there, with her friends, showing the world what she was made of.

In that moment, she even thought that it might be better than cooking!

Madame Ruby swept up to the stage to address the audience.

'Ladies and gentlemen. Thank you so very much for joining us this afternoon for what I'm sure you'll agree has been the most incredible journey around the world in forty minutes!'

The audience clapped again.

'As you all know, we've been very lucky indeed to be joined by Princess Ameera this term and I'm delighted to tell you that her parents are with us this afternoon and would like to say a few words.' She motioned for Ameera's parents to join her.

'Good afternoon, everyone. What a wonderful performance. Congratulations to everyone involved, none more so than our Ameera,' Prince Imran began.

Ameera thought she might faint.

'It's not only Ameera who will take away a few lessons from her wonderful time here at L'Etoile, but my wife and I too. Life is so precious and is nothing if it isn't enjoyed to the full.'

'Oh my goodness,' Pippa whispered in the darkness of the stage.

'Ameera, girls, won't you join us?' said Princess

Preeti, looking behind her for a glimpse of her daughter.

Ameera came out of the shadows and, quite forgetting royal protocol, ran to her mother for a hug.

Luscious Tangerella, who'd rushed to L'Etoile after Maria's phone call and was now standing at the side of the stage with her top photographer (with permission from Madame Ruby and Prince Imran of course!) launched forward amid an explosion of camera flashes. This was a truly huge scoop for her. Catching a never-before-seen image of the Indian royal family in such an emotional moment would mean worldwide fame and fortune for the *Gazette* and she was delighted! All thanks to little Maria!

'Things are going to be different, my darling, I promise you,' Princess Preeti said lovingly to her only daughter.

Ameera could do nothing but cling to her mother with happiness.

As her father continued to thank everyone in the room, Ameera looked over to her girls – her friends – and blew them a kiss.

Molly had been quite right. *Dreams really do come true at L'Etoile.*

A Guide to Molly Fitzfoster's Favourite Sayings

OOTW = Out Of This World

CAAC = Cool As A Cucumber

ICBI = I Can't Bear It

GMTA = Great Minds Think Alike

OMG = Oh My Goodness

WFIN = We're For It Now

TDF = To Die For

WATC = What Are The Chances?

IIH = I'm In Heaven

*Join the girls for more fabulous fun-filled
adventures in the School for Stars series . . .*

First Term at L'Etoile

On the first day of term at L'Etoile, School for Stars,
twins Maria and Molly Fitzfoster meet
Pippa Burrows who's won a song-writing
scholarship to the school. The talented trio share
the same dreams of super-stardom and become best
friends. But will their friendship stand up against
Lucifette Marciano's plans to wreck their chances
and claim fame for herself?

978 1 4440 0811 1

£4.99

Second Term at L'Etoile

The Christmas holidays are over and best friends Molly, Maria and Pippa return to their beloved L'Etoile, School for Stars for more fun and adventure. A midnight hunt for lost treasure, a playful puppy with a twinkle in her eye and a royal visit are just some of the things they're about to share. They may be friends forever, but will they make it to the end of term without getting expelled?

978 1 4440 0813 5

£4.99

Third Term at L'Etoile

Our favourite friends forever are back for another exciting term. A television show comes to school and plans are afoot for a glittering end of term charity fundraiser. But as you know, Story-seeker, there's never an adventure without a drama at L'Etoile, and with Molly's Hollywood audition, the dreaded summer exams and the return of Lucifette Marciano with her truly hideous friend, we're just not sure how the girls are going to survive . . .

978 1 4440 0815 9

£4.99

Summer Holiday Mystery

Molly and Maria fly home from Hollywood
for a rest, but their summer holiday by the sea
with Pippa and Sally is anything but relaxing!
Strange howling noises in the night, a disappearing
puppy, a secret cave and kidnap lead the four
BFFs on a hair-raising adventure. But will they
solve the mystery in time to save the day?

978 1 4440 0817 3

£4.99

Double Trouble at L'Etoile

Molly, Maria, Pippa and Sally are all set for their
second year at L'Etoile, School for Stars. After the
excitement of their first year and holiday adventures
they've promised their parents an event-free term.
But we all know that's not going to happen, don't
we? A new pair of twins in school and some ghostly
goings-on mean the BFFs have to get their skates on
to solve a spooky mystery.

978 1 4440 1455 6

£5.99

The Missing Ballerina Mystery

After a busy term at L'Etoile, it's time for a London holiday. But adventure follows the BFFs wherever they go, and it's not long before they find themselves exploring hidden tunnels and buried secrets surrounding a missing ballerina. Here's a mystery to really keep them on their toes!

978 1 4440 1457 0

£5.99

the
orion star

CALLING ALL GROWN-UPS!
Sign up for **the orion star** newsletter to
hear about your favourite authors and exclusive
competitions, plus details of how children
can join our 'Story Stars' review panel.

Sign up at:

www.orionbooks.co.uk/orionstar

Follow us 🐦 @the_orionstar
Find us 📘 facebook.com/TheOrionStar